Charity

Mail Order Brides of Wichita Falls

CYNDI RAYE

Charity
Mail Order Brides
of
Wichita Falls
Book 4
by
Cyndi Raye

---

1. http://www.CyndiRaye.com

Chapter 1

Charity marched up the two flights of stairs to the smokey offices in the three story building in the center of Chicago's business district. The Chicago Tribute was ripe and rolling with hard core male news reporters and a bevy of professional men who would stomp across the next reporters back to get the story of the hour. Not one person acknowledged her in this man's world.

She slipped through the door to stand in front of an oversized desk cluttered with newspapers and dried coffee stains dotting the mess. *This is it! After two years working those horrible assignments, I'm finally going to be promoted!*

Charity stood inside the door, her chin in the air. She smoothed her skirts with delicate hands trying not to show how nervous she was inside. A knowing smile kept interfering with the stoic look she was trying to present to Barry Simms, the general manager of the newspaper. She had been offered a chance to show her true skills last week when a fire broke out in one of the major department stores. For the last few days she barely slept, investigating the fire, talking to neighbors and eye witnesses who claimed to have seen someone leaving the building right before it burst into flames. Charity had been the first reporter to interview the witness, the only reporter to get the whole story. That had to account for something. Now they were so close to finding the culprit and her story could reach out to others that may know who the instigator was as she had an eye witness accounting of the whole thing.

She usually was sent to the women's sewing circle, or a gardening expedition to report on the types of flowers that grew in certain soils. It wasn't the type of hard core reporting Charity wanted to do. As a woman, she knew she'd have to work harder and smarter to move up in the ranks of newsworthy reporters, which happened to be crowded with men.

Today was the day to prove herself. After she had handed in her prize article yesterday, she had gone home to an empty apartment to pace the floor most of the evening. Her room mate was out celebrating her last day in Chicago. Sleep evaded her, instead, dreams of being cast aside peppered her thoughts. Yet, when she realized she had first dibbs at the top reporter position, she forged ahead, deciding it didn't matter if she were a woman but what mattered was she told a great story. They would see it, they had to. Obviously, someone did see her potential as she was called to the top managers office the moment she walked in the door this morning. Now here she stood in front of Barry Simms.

Trying not to show nerves of any sort one way or the other, Charity clasped her hands behind her back, standing as tall as was humanly possible. "Good morning, sir."

Barry leaned back in his padded chair, the rollers on the legs making a creepy squeaking sound as he pushed the chair back against the wall. He stared hard.

She got the impression he was angry. Since this was the first time she actually came face to face with this man of high position, Charity decided to steel herself and smile. It was a matter of principle for her. No matter what happened, she would never let anyone see her get emotional. A dull ache began in her belly. She had an instant suspicion this wasn't about the promotion, not with the look of anger on the man's face.

She decided to get to the point. "Did I do something wrong, sir?"

He continued to stare. His jaw dropped, making a clicking noise right before he picked up her report and handed it back to her.

Charity stiffened her back before taking it from his hand. Looking down, her brow furrowed. "This is my report. I'm assuming you didn't like what you read?"

Barry reached across his desk to another pile of papers. Picking one from the top, he handed it to her. "Read the by-line and the first paragraph."

She did. "Sir?"

"Who is the reporter named on the piece you are holding?"

"Jimmy Fallstown." Charity scanned the piece with observant eyes, not believing what she was reading. "It can't be! This was stolen," she claimed, fury spreading over her face. "Stolen, from me," she added.

"Perhaps you can explain to me why your same report is exactly as Jimmys?"

"He stole it, that conniving little creep!"

Barry grunted. He stood up, towering over Charity like a hangman's noose. "I gave you a chance to prove yourself, Miss Johnson. I was almost sure you would give me a good report. Almost had me convinced a woman could do a man's job." He shook his head back and forth, obviously disappointed.

Charity snapped her head back, looking up at him with blue eyes the color of sapphires. She threw the report back on his desk. "Mine is not fraudulent. I wrote that piece and my name shall be on it, so help me, God." She crossed her arms over herself and stared hard at Barry Simms. General manager or not, she had to convince him that Jimmy Fallstown was the fraud, not her.

"Jimmy's been here a long time, Miss Johnson. Calling him a fraud isn't a smart move to the top."

"Why? Because he stole my paper I worked hard on, I should sit back and accept this because I am a woman? The man's gotten lazy. Look at him?" She turned and pointed to the window where the hub of reporter's desks could be seen in the large rectangular area. Jimmy leaned casually back in his seat, sipping coffee and reading a newspaper, arrogant as all get out.

"You can't be accusing a man like him of stealing your work. How in the world could he steal this? It was here on my desk from the time you handed it in yesterday."

Charity fumed. She tipped her head to the side and stared right back at Barry Simms. "I want you to call him in here. Let's see what he has to say."

"No."

"Do it or I will."

"Words like that will get you fired."

"I'm probably fired anyway. I want him to know I am on to him. Call him."

Barry sighed. He turned to the large picture window and rapped on the glass. Many heads turned but he pointed to Jimmy and waved him in. It didn't take long for the skinny reporter to knock on the glass door.

"Enter."

Jimmy smiled sweetly at Charity as if he didn't just steal her whole livelihood.

She stared at him with all the contempt and anger mustered from deep inside.

"How can I help you, boss?" Jimmy took a seat opposite Barry, who was still standing behind his own desk.

"Miss Johnson appears to have the same report as you. What do you have to say?"

"Charity? You copied from me?" His words grated on her ears because he didn't seem at all surprised. She wanted to take the smirk right off his face. If she weren't a woman, she would give him a punch in the gut. Hard. Grinding her teeth together so she wouldn't cry out at what a snake he was, she sucked in a deep breath and tried to stay calm.

"I know you stole my work, Jimmy. I don't know how you managed to accomplish such a task, but I suggest you tell Mr. Simms the truth."

Jimmy acted affronted. "I'll do no such thing. I'm afraid you stopping at my desk every day for the last few days proved to be unsettling now that I think about things. You were pretending to be nice and all you wanted was to steal *my* project. How dare *you*?"

Charity's hands went to her hips. "Is that all the better you can do? I'll be right back." Leaving the two, she hurried down the steps, rushing to her cubicle where her draft copy of the report laid under a ransacked pile of papers. She snatched it up and hurried back upstairs, ignoring the stares that followed. The smell of strong coffee wafted in the air. Keys from typewriters chirped as other reporters worked on their own pieces. She firmly closed the door, drowning out the noise.

Walking over to the general managers desk, she ignored the smirk on Jimmy's face. "Sir? Here is my draft."

"You stole my draft, too? Impossible what some new reporters will do to best me."

She turned. "This draft is mine." She handed it to Barry. "Look at it. I circle all my corrections and initial each page." She pointed to the letters C and J in the right lower corner of the pages.

Barry turned each page, looking through the paper. Relief surged through the coarse of her veins. As he stared at the draft, she turned to Jimmy, raising a brow in his direction. The smirk never left his face as he shrugged his shoulders and pushed himself deeper into the chair.

When she turned back to Barry he was holding the papers out to her. She took them back and smiled. "Well?"

He shook his head. "I'm sorry, Miss Johnson. This draft tells me nothing. Jimmy has been here a long, long time. You've been here two years. I have to believe that he is telling the truth."

"But my initials are right here! Are you daft?" Charity knew those words would get her fired but her temper was getting the upper hand. How could a reasonable and intelligent man miss the point?

When she stared in his eyes she saw the pity there. Pity for her? She didn't want his pity, she wanted a chance that she deserved. Her paper was one of the best articles she had ever written. "This isn't fair," she told him again. "How can you not acknowledge that I am the true owner of this article?"

Barry stammered a bit but then his shoulders went back and he stared hard at her. "Miss Johnson, I'm afraid in light of all this, I'm going to have to let you go. I can't have you stealing another man's reports. As a woman reporter, this won't look good for your kind at all."

For her kind? She sputtered. "The hell you say? For your information, I quit, you can't fire me!" With that, she ripped the good report from his desk and turned on her heels. Picking up her skirts, Charity stopped when she reached Jimmy. "Charity Johnson. Remember that name," she told him between gritted teeth. She stomped to the door and flung it open. "You would be best to remember because someday I'll be bigger and more famous than little Jimmy Fallstown, the has-been lame reporter that can't write his own work. You wait and see!"

The apartment was cold and lonely when Charity finally got home. She lit the oil lamps, pacing the floor of their tiny, two bedroom hole in the wall where she and her best friend, Samantha Malone, had lived for the last few years. The two had been together in college. Charity learning how to become a reporter and Sami, as she like to be called, graduated from the school of nursing. The two became fast friends after taking a class together and decided to share the expenses of this tiny apartment along the river. Now Sami was moving on, getting married to a stranger she had never met somewhere out west and Charity would be alone.

Without a job.

For the last two weeks she had tried to find a job as a reporter but every single news office refused to hire a woman. She would have to fix things before her entire savings was used up in rent since Sami would be leaving tomorrow and the rent was due in five days. She may be able to pay for a few months but after that, if she didn't find work, she'd be homeless.

The door knob turned and Sami flew through the door, her impeccable smile changing Charity's mood. Sami had that effect on everyone she came in contact with.

"I'm so excited!" She told Charity. "I'm sad to leave you but look at what Mr. Good sent me." She held out the envelope for Charity to take.

Charity's eyes widened when she saw the pile of cash inside. "He sent you this?"

"Yes, so I don't have to spend my own money on the trip. He's paid for a train ticket and all my meals. I can't wait to meet him!"

Charity hugged her friend. "I'm so happy for you. Are you sure this is what you want?"

Her friend wrapped her arms around Charity and sniffled. "I will miss you so much. The man is a doctor and he needs a nurse for his growing practice. It's the perfect opportunity for me to do good. From what I understand the growing town is in terrible need of medical assistance. I can't wait to go there and show them what I learned."

"I know you will be a wonderful nurse. I will miss you terribly."

Sami smiled through a bevy of tears. "I wish you would think about what I said."

Charity stepped back. "I am not sure what you mean?"

"Here." Sami reached for the paper sitting on a small desk along the wall. "I kept this for you. Go ahead and read it, who knows, you may find someone who will accompany your deepest wishes and desires."

"Oh, Sami, that sounds like a proposition!"

The two giggled.

"Promise me, Charity, that you will at least consider becoming a mail order bride."

The thought made her cringe. "I don't want to be attached to someone I don't know! Why, what if they turned out like the men at the Chicago Tribute? Men so arrogant who don't think a woman can do anything except cook and clean and keep their beds warm?"

Sami smiled. "Oh, Charity, no wonder you are a newswoman. Your imagination is so wild! There are plenty of men looking for a wife for other reasons as well. They are looking for a partner, someone that will help them in their chosen field. Perhaps you can find someone like that, a newsman worthy of you."

"I doubt a man like that exists outside of your imagination, Sami."

She shrugged. "Look at me then, Charity. I do believe I've found the man of my dreams. We've been writing back and forth for months now. He is kind and gentle and a doctor who is well respected. The owner of the mail order bride agency investigates everyone listed in her directory. She won't put anyone in there who is a fraud. Trust me on this. It may be the only way you can ever become a newsworthy reporter in this day and age. You've got so much against you here in Chicago."

"You're not kidding, Sami. I'm done in this town. No one will hire me. I guess maybe I'll take a look."

Excitement shown in her friend's eyes as they made supper together in the kitchen for the last time. They both grabbed a plate and scoured the want ads as they settled at the small wooden table against the wall of the tiny kitchen.

Sami began to read some of the ads. "I am 40 years young and tired of the bachelor life. Looking for a woman not over 20 who can cook, clean and not ugly. Well educated and who has at least twenty thousand dollars of her own money."

Charity shook her head. "Forget it, too old."

"Here's another. Aged 28, dark hair and eyes and considered handsome by former girlfriends. Looking for someone who likes to have fun while keeping house and desires to take care of 4 children."

"Not for me."

"Okay, here. How about this one," Sami told her, obvious frustration in her tone. "Man of means looking for not only a partner but a hard worker. Will consider marriage after one year of working my farm."

Charity laughed out loud. "Oh, Sami. Stop. If I want someone I'll make my own advertisement and put it in the paper. I can write an advertisement much better than any of these."

Sami's head snapped up from the paper. "That's perfect. Let's write a letter to an intended groom of what you want and when you see me off at the train station tomorrow morning, stop by Angela Brown's Agency. She'll take care of the rest, find you the perfect partner and mate."

They spent the next few hours compiling a letter to be sent to a man looking for a bride who didn't want to be a bride but who wanted to further her career. Charity was shocked she let Sami convince her to go through with this, but if her instincts were right, she'd have to do something drastic. Soon. Her money would be gone in a few weeks and without a job, there was nothing keeping her here in Chicago any longer.

Chapter 2

"I'vve already written a letter confirming my availability. There isn't much time to waste, so I took it upon myself to do so." Charity stood face to face with the owner of the Angel Matchmaking Agency Sami had sent her to. The same one who found Sami a groom she was about to meet up with in a few days.

"Thank you. It certainly will save time. You say you are a newspaper woman?"

Charity nodded to the beautiful lady standing there. She had silky dark hair, almost black, set in a long braid that hung over one shoulder in a romantic way. Her flowing skirts were feminine and made of expensive silk. The thought occurred to Charity there may be a story here. Why would such a beautiful women be hiding in a store front office matching women with partners out west?

"You are wondering why I am doing this?"

Charity grinned. "Yes." She was always honest and strait to the point and didn't like people to lie. It made her a great reporter but as a person, it sometimes offended others.

Angela Brown scanned Charity's letter. She lifted her chin and smiled, a dimple in the left cheek. "Perhaps someday I will tell you my story. But not today."

"Promise?" Charity asked. She wanted first chance at this woman's life story. Most of all she wanted to know what made the other woman do this kind of work. "I think your situation may be an interesting story to write about."

Mrs. Brown smiled sadly. "I'm afraid you are right. But, we are not here to talk about me. There is a businessman in the small, growing Texas town of Wichita Falls who is perhaps looking for a bride. I recently received a telegram from a local agency there who is in need of finding him a mate right away. If you wouldn't mind changing a few items in this letter, I'll send this out immediately."

Charity didn't say anything at first. Was she ready to go through with marrying some stranger in a small town so far from where she grew up? She looked out the window of the store front. The streets were bustling with men and women, some stopping to purchase items where shop keepers and others were selling their wares. Chicago was growing fast and hard and by the looks of things, she'd have to continue to fight her way to the top. That's if anyone hired her. She had been at every single newspaper in town. So far no one would consider hiring a woman.

"Miss Johnson?"

Charity sighed. "Hand me the letter and tell me what you want changed."

Mrs. Brown did so, getting up and leaning over Charity's shoulder to help with the wording of a few sentences. When she was finished, she laid the pencil back down and flexed her fingers. "That's it, how soon will I hear something?"

"How desperate are you, Charity?"

"I can't find work. In two weeks my funds run out and I'll be homeless. There's no work for a woman, not even factory work. The city has an over-abundance of workers right now. I went to the employment agency to find out it could be months before a job opens up."

"I see. Well, then, Charity, I'll expedite this letter and ask for a prompt reply. We should know something by next week."

Charity got up from her seat, feeling unsatisfied. She hated the desperation in her heart and soul. It wasn't how she was made. Forcing herself to marry someone to get what she wanted, a job, was the worst thing ever. Yet, there was still a fighting chance someone would hire her here in Chicago before she took this offer. Besides, she promised that little rat, Jimmy, her name would be bigger than his someday. How could she do so thousands of miles away? Confusion and anxiety filled her heart.

"Thank you." She made to leave when Mrs. Brown placed a hand on her sleeve.

"I have an idea. I'm so busy that I've been working late into the night. I would like to hire you temporarily to help write some advertisements. Would you be willing to do so for an hourly wage?"

"My name may be Charity, but I don't take charity."

Mrs. Brown smiled, her dimple setting deep in her cheek. "I don't expect you to sit around here all day doing nothing. Trust me, you will be working your fingers to the bone. I have more work here than one person can handle. Will I see you in the morning?"

"Yes. Of course." Charity didn't want her to see the look of relief on her face so she hurried to the front door of the office. "Thank you." She scurried out the door and down the steps, finally breaking out in a big smile. At least she had a temporary job until the businessman responded to her letter. Her steps were lighter as she headed down the side walk. Instead of turning towards her lonely apartment, Charity took a route that led to the city park. It was too lovely a day to be inside.

<> <>

Clutching the letter from the mail order bride in his hand, he ignored Ben Sloan when the man got up to leave. Uncurling the wrinkled letter, he laid it out in front of him. Pushing his much-needed glasses up the bridge of his nose, he focused on the woman's fancy writing. His close friend, Ben, the owner of the finest hotel in Wichita Falls, had no intention of sending for a mail order bride. It had been a ruse to make his true love jealous. Daniel, on the other hand, had every intention of finding a partner.

Dear Sir, I was asked to send a letter to you in hopes there could be a union of sorts between the two of us. I want to add I am a very independent woman with a career. I love my work more than anything and if I do take up your offer of marriage as a mail order bride, it is my sole intention to continue to work in my chosen field as a newspaper reporter. You must know this up front before any type of matrimony occurs. I am not too tall of a woman, have dark hair and love to investigate all kinds of events. I am a curious sort who loves to indulge in the mystery of things. If you, sir, need someone to cook, clean and be a child bearer, then I am not for you. I am blunt and to the point and want you to be the same. My intentions of becoming a mail order bride is to carve out a career out west where men don't push women out of the way like they do here in Chicago. I am educated but can't get a decent job for the life of me in this city as a news reporter, and understand you are a businessman who understands my intentions. If you, sir, are indeed interested in more, please send a letter as soon as possible as I am fully intending to go through with any offer that will help to move my career forward. Yours truly, Charity Johnson

Perfect! Daniel Ashwood grinned. He rubbed a hand over his jaw, realizing the stubble that grew there from ignoring his own daily habits. He'd have to no doubt shave to make himself presentable but that wasn't a problem. He'd take a trip over to Lii, the towns only barber, to clean up his act. Perhaps spend a few coins on one of those fancy showers in the hotel his friend, Ben, owned. It wasn't that he was dirty, no. He had so much work running a newspaper that it would be days sometimes before he'd go upstairs and clean up.

Daniel had deadlines like any other newspaper in the territory. Except he was striving to make his the best ever, giving more value for their five cents than any other paper. Whatever he was doing worked. People stood in line waiting for the weekly paper to come out. Filled with stories, true and bold about Indians, frontier life and his weekly fiction serial, *Outlaw Stories*, along with local advertisements, even farmers living miles from town made an extra trip on Monday morning to buy the paper.

A woman reporter would be a perfect wife. She didn't want babies or any of the household duties a normal wife should do. That would be easy to accommodate as long as she helped him with the newspaper. He had a small apartment on the second floor. It wasn't much but he didn't need much. Besides, Daniel cared about one thing. His newspaper. It was his life, what he lived for, writing the news. Ever since his parents abandoned him as an infant at the home for wayward children in New York City, he was determined to plant roots in Wichita Falls. Perhaps riding the Orphan Train at eleven years old was the best thing that ever happened to him.

The thick dust in his apartment upstairs was not a big deal. He'd hire someone from town to swipe over the place before his future bride got here. Taking a sheet of fresh stationary from his desk, Daniel began the task of writing the best introductory letter ever before getting back to work.

<> <>

Charity waved a gloved hand to her new friend and ex-employer through the cloudy window of the Union Pacific car. Her things were all packed, labelled and delivered to the cargo department. Charity was shocked herself at all the things she had accumulated in the last two years. Two trunks and a carpetbag stuffed full with her belongings would be taking this trip with her. She had been so busy making a name for herself, which clearly didn't happen, Charity hadn't realized she had bought so many outfits from fine department stores in Chicago. Most of her pay went to rent, food and nice outfits for assignments. Even if they weren't the best in the world, Charity liked to look sparkling, sharp and professional.

She arranged the edge of her skirt neatly over her ankles as it had worked its way up her legs when she sat on the seat. Scooting closer to the window, Charity watched the skyline of Chicago go by, a bitter-sweet smile portraying the mood she was in. She would have been a great reporter there, she mused. If only.

But this was a new chapter of her life and she wasn't about to drown in sorrow and sadness or let anything or anyone stop her from this moment on. It was said in the west anyone could become whatever they wanted to be. There were freedoms out beyond the mountains and prairies unheard of east of the Mississippi and she was aiming to find out.

She had to prove to herself and to those scrupulous men back in Chicago that Charity Johnson was not a garden-party reporter but a top-notch news reporter. She would become the most notorious newswoman in the west.

Pulling out a pencil and paper from an overstuffed reticule, Charity wasn't about to relax. She wanted to record every sound, smell and movement of her trip riding the rails. When she published her excursion westward, she wanted the readers to feel as if they went with her on this journey. It would make a fine story for the newspaper. After miles of putting pen to paper, the chug-chug-chug of the car lulled her to sleep. She dropped her chin in her chest and let the pencil fall to her lap.

Charity woke with a start. She placed a gloved hand over her mouth before emitting a loud yawn so long it scrunched up the features of her pretty face. The edge of her hat had tipped to one side and she carefully moved it back in place.

"It's time to eat supper, you know," an anonymous voice said behind her seat. She turned to find a little man whose feet didn't touch the floor staring at her, a big smile on his friendly face. He had a dark beard and moustache that turned up at the ends.

Charity swallowed. "Hello. I don't believe I've had the pleasure of your name, sir?" Her hand swung out to take his in a firm handshake.

"Name's Mr. Martin."

"Why, hello, Mr. Martin. I am Miss Johnson." She stood up to go to the dining car, realizing she was indeed hungry. He scooted off of his seat and held out his arm.

"It would be a pleasure to have you dine with us?"

Charity rarely missed a thing. "Us?" She gazed beside him and behind but there was no one else.

"My wife and I. She is already at a table. I thought I would wait for you to finish napping to invite you to dinner."

Charity took his small arm with her hand, finding it interesting to know someone had taken an interest in her. "Lead the way, sir, I am famished."

She learned over the course of the meal Mr. and Mrs. Martin travelled quite often from Chicago to Fort Worth and other places as well. At first Mr. Martin didn't want to give anything away but through her persistent questioning, she found out he was a wealthy man who loved to travel and the railroad was his means of doing business, investing in the railroad of course and many other business ventures along the way. It was impossible to say what all he owned his wife told Charity in the rare moment she spoke up.

"What is the West like?" Charity asked, curious to hear from someone who had been there.

"Oh my dear, what a loaded question. The West is filled with vast lands that are so empty in some areas you won't see a settlement for many, many miles. All of a sudden you will come upon a town in the middle of nowhere. The railroad is becoming the popular way to travel now-a-days, ever since the connection at Promontory. Why, I have rode the rails from Boston to California."

"Do you mind if I interview you, Mr. Martin? I am a reporter."

A smile spread across his miniature cheeks. He blushed. "A reporter? Yes, yes, of course. Just ask away and I'll tell you what I know." His wife nudged him with her elbow. She hadn't said much with her mouth full of the food from her supper plate. Mrs. Martin liked to eat.

For the next hour and a half, Charity sat in the dining car listening to Mr. Martin and his tales of travel to the west. She hurried to write down every detail, making sure not to miss anything of importance. The rest she would have to keep in her memory. "Thank you for your kindness," she told him as they parted ways. "This adventure story will be in the first publication, I promise."

As the next two days sped by, Charity became more excited the closer she got to Texas. Stopping and picking up passengers or dropping off folks at stations along the way kept the train from moving along in a timely fashion. Even so, there was plenty to observe along the way. Charity introduced herself to several strangers she thought may add intrigue and a bit of excitement to her story she planned to present to her new husband, who hopefully would allow her the freedom of publishing any article she wanted.

She pondered her new life as the wife of man who owned a newspaper. What would he be like? Scatter-brained like some of those reporters in Chicago? Or a hard-core women hater? The thought made her skin crawl for a moment as she gazed over the prairie from the window. Was she trading one job for another that wouldn't be any better?

Charity pulled out the letter he had sent, reading it over for the tenth time.

Dear Miss Johnson, I am not the businessman you originally intended to write to but in all consideration, I would like to plead my case. The original owner of this letter has reconsidered a mail order bride because of issues of his concern. To be honest and between the two of us, his intentions were only for a dark-haired beauty here in our small town of Wichita Falls. It is a love story at best and if you agree to my proposition, I will enlighten you of this wonderful romance in person.

I find this is a perfect opportunity for the both of us. I run the only newspaper in Wichita Falls and am in desperate need of help. As a news woman, I truly believe you would be the perfect partner to help me run things here. I've hired local people but they never work out, losing interest in the newsworthy assignments too quickly. I am offering you a hand in marriage but there is one condition and that is to be my faithful wife in all areas except the following: no cooking, cleaning or household work. No waiting on a husband hand and foot. I need a professional news reporter to make my newspaper the best in the area. Would you accept my proposal?

I find I'm not a romantic at heart and don't know how to do romance but I will be the best partner in the world of business. Please accept this money to purchase a train ticket right away. If you don't mind sending a telegraph as soon as possible, I'll make the preparations for everything so you will literally walk in the door and get to work at what it sounds like you love doing. Sincerely, Daniel Ashwood.

It did sound heavenly! To be able to walk in the door and begin working in the job of her dreams! Charity sighed. Her talent at writing stories would be known in the town of Wichita Falls. Even if it wasn't a popular town, it was a start. She had to be sure this man was not a fraud and everything he claimed to be.

One more night on the train and she'd be in her new home.

Chapter 3

Daniel clicked open the stopwatch to find himself behind again. In less than an hour, his new bride would be here. He had to finish the story. Just another ten minutes should do. Pushing his dark framed glasses back up, he bent over the desk and began to scribble as fast as possible.

Someone shuffled down the steps slowly, opened the hallway door and popped their head inside the newsroom. "Daniel?" a voice whispered.

His head reluctantly came up to see who was annoying him. "What is it?"

"Sorry to bother you but I must get back home. I'm sure the children are getting restless. I know you didn't ask for supper but I have some pot luck warming on your stove."

Mrs. Fisher was a sweet lady. Daniel felt ashamed. He stood and walked towards her as he pulled bills from his pocket. "I'm sorry, Mrs. Fisher, I didn't mean to sound annoyed. Thank you for cleaning my place up."

She accepted the money from his outstretched hand and tucked it in her breast pocket, smiling. Daniel thought she looked tired. The woman normally had boundless energy for being in her fifties. She took care of four grandchildren and her husband, who lost his leg in the war. Her daughter and son-in-law died a few years back in a wagon accident making her the sole guardian of the four small children. She took on extra chores cleaning houses and doing whatever it took to make ends meet. Daniel always called her even if he didn't need much more than an errand run. Even though he needed to get back to his project, he tried to be kind with small talk. "How are the children?"

"They are wonderful, Mr. Daniel. The oldest boy, Thomas, plans to become a news reporter, just like you. He says he will be famous!" She cackled at the remark, pushing some gray hair from her forehead.

Daniel noticed how her hands shook. He dug deeper in his pockets. "Here."

She shook her head and stepped back. "No, Mr. Daniel, that is unacceptable. I work hard for my wages and will not take a hand-out." Anger flashed across her face.

"Mrs. Fisher. I'm not giving you charity. I would like to hire your son for one hour a day to help me and this is the first weeks pay. Take a look around, I need all the help I can get." There was clutter everywhere, she couldn't deny that fact.

She lowered her head to stare at him with aging eyes. "You sure about that? I thought that was why you were getting yourself a mail order bride?"

He shrugged and pushed the money in her hand, closing her fist. She didn't hand it back but stuffed it in her pocket with the rest. Daniel sighed deeply. He had enough money to hire a young man who obviously wanted to learn the tricks of the trade. Having an apprentice would benefit the paper. "She is a reporter like me and will be too busy to do some of the small tasks that I am hiring your grandson for. He can start at the bottom and learn the trade. Do we have an agreement?"

"Welp, I guess we do as long as Thomas agrees. I better be on my way. You best finish up and get to the depot. Train will be here in about ten minutes."

Daniel heard the bell above the front door jingle as he ran full speed ahead up the stairs, taking two at a time. He stopped in his tracks when he saw what a little housecleaning could do to an untidy place. Mrs. Fisher had dusted and swept, even opened a window to clear the air. A single flower in a vase sat on the small table pushed up against the window. Along with the smell of dinner, the place seemed a bit cozy and romantic. He laughed out loud. No one in their right mind would accuse him of being romantic.

Daniel dipped his head and cupped his hands, filling them with the water from the wash basin. He scrubbed his hands across his face, taking the hanging towel and drying his skin. As he pulled the towel from his face, he caught his reflection in the mirror hanging above the basin. It was the first time he had gazed at himself in a long, long time.

Dark hair stood up everywhere without rhyme or reason. Daniel chuckled at himself at the comical way he looked. Was this how everyone saw him? He reminded himself of the madman in an old classic story he read once. He found a brush on the bedside table, wetting it a bit before combing it through the mess. He went to put his glasses back on and hesitated. He looked way better without the dark monsters framing his eyes. Sliding them in a breast pocket, Daniel took the palm of his hand over his chin. Tiny whiskers stood out but he didn't have time to shave. He never shaved until he had to so why should he start now? The bride-to-be would either have to be satisfied with the way he looked or she could get back on the train and head east.

The shrewd whistle of the train had him checking his stop watch one more time. It couldn't be possible ten minutes had gone by already! But that was Daniel's life, the minutes ticked away and he was never on time unless it benefited the newspaper. Realizing Miss Johnson would benefit the newspaper had him hurrying back downstairs and out the door.

There was a hustle in the air that always happened when the train pulled in. Townsfolk scurried to the depot to catch the train that only stayed no more than twenty minutes. Daniel fell in beside a couple who was leaving Wichita Falls for good. They grumbled about the dusty town, claiming it was much better in the East.

Daniel needed to interview them. "Excuse me, please. Do you have a moment to talk to me. I run the Wichita Falls newspaper and have a few questions about your stay here."

The couple slowed down at the opportunity of an interview. "You'll have to walk with us. We have to catch the train before it leaves."

Daniel dug in his pocket for pen and paper. He hurdled questions as they went to the train depot, slower than usual. Most of the passengers that got off the train were already gone by the time he approached the platform. Keeping his head down, Daniel scribbled on his paper as quickly as possible.

"We must be going," the wife announced, hurrying towards the car.

"Thanks for the interview. I didn't get your names."

"John and Mary Stewart," the young man called back. "You can quote me on anything I said. Good riddance to the West!"

As Daniel wrote down the last words, he heard a dainty cough. Looking up, he realized he was no longer alone. A petite lady stood in the depot, staring at him with blazing eyes. Angry, yet curious eyes.

With a reporter's eye, he gazed over her frame from the top of her dark, almost black hair to the tips of patent leather boots sticking out from her skirts. She dressed well, looked like she took good care of herself. When he looked back up in to those sapphire eyes, her stare was steady. She hadn't flinched when he looked her over. "I assume you must be Miss Johnson?"

Her nod was barely audible. She was studying him with the same boldness and regard he had just done to her. Bravo! he thought. She wasn't a shy one. She stared boldly in his hazel eyes right before she slowly let her gaze wonder down the length of him. Daniel didn't mind a bit. His body began to wake up and remind him a woman hadn't looked at him like this in a long, long time. If they did, he never noticed with his head in the news business day and night.

"Do you like what you see?" he asked, his low tone catching her attention. She took a step back at first before breaking out in to a big smile.

She placed a hand on her hip. "Do you want me to lie or to be honest?"

He laughed, his eyes crinkling a bit at the edges. "Honesty is the best policy."

She smiled again, avoiding the answer. "That's an old cliché."

They stood there for a few more minutes, making small talk, oblivious to anyone else. The fervor going on in those blue eyes put Daniel in a frenzy. All of a sudden he had a yearning to pull her into his arms and kiss those soft lips.

The pull was so strong he almost did when she mentioned they should have her trunks moved. Daniel snapped out of the trance she was putting him in. His body was not reacting well. This was supposed to be a business arrangement. Nothing else. He had a paper to run, he couldn't afford to be distracted.

"Leave the trunks, we have to meet at the church for our ceremony in ten minutes. May I escort you?"

The surprise on her face made him grin. "I'm not leaving my trunks behind." With that announcement, she plopped down on the one trunk and crossed her arms. Looking up at him, she glared. "Are you laughing at me, sir?"

Daniel didn't want to scare her off, even if he didn't think she would scare so easily. "I've hired someone to get your things for you. Here he is now." One of the young men working at the train depot pulled a horse and wagon up just in time.

"Oh!" She didn't blush but her cheeks pinkened a bit. Daniel acted as if he didn't notice. In a ladylike fashion, Miss Johnson picked up her skirts and stood, taking the few steps to where Daniel waited. She pointedly glared at his arm, the one he held out to her earlier. Another tiny cough got his attention.

Another grin followed as he held out his arm once again. "My pleasure, Miss Johnson. Shall we proceed to the church?"

She tilted her head to one side, clutching her hand tighter around his arm. "May as well get that part over with."

"It won't be that bad," he told her, amused at the loathing in her voice. Sounding as if she were being gagged and tied and forced to marry, he shook his head. "Pretend you are having fun at least."

A look of understanding came over her. She placed her other hand on his arm. Daniel was surprised at the instant heat coming from her gloved hands. And from him. This wasn't supposed to happen. He couldn't help himself as he turned and cupped her chin, brushing a thumb over her soft skin. He moved closer, his body betraying it's own reasoning. The fervor in her eyes told him a different story all together. She didn't relish the idea of having to get married, he realized that much. But she had passion and zeal and he could feel it in her spirit.

The thought struck him that maybe they could have it all. He looked deep in those orbs and was lost. Leaning in, he brushed her mouth with his, so softly he swore she sighed. "You fascinate me, Miss Johnson," he said as he brushed over her mouth once again.

She pulled away. "I did not come here for this," she whispered, her voice trembling.

"I can't seem to help myself," he admitted, hoping that would calm her fears. It only enraged her more.

"Mr. Ashwood, am I going to be pawned on and man-handled for the duration of my marriage to you? I distinctly agreed to a business arrangement first and foremost!"

Daniel stopped short. "Miss Johnson, your words speak a different language than your actions. If I recall," he said, lowering his mouth to her ear, "you didn't move away when I brushed my mouth over yours." With that, he placed a soft kiss on her cheek and held out his other hand. "Shall we?"

He watched in amusement as she took the steps to the street, staying clear of getting too close even though her arm was in his. The bustle of her traveling dress swayed as she moved with ease through the streets of Wichita Falls. He watched as her curious eyes didn't miss a thing. Passing the salon Daniel thought she would be fearful but that was furtherest from her mind. She walked slower, straining her neck a bit to try to see in to the saloon itself.

Daniel chuckled. It was going to be an interesting marriage for sure. He slowed when they came upon the town's hotel. "I have to let our witnesses know we are ready. We'll be but a minute," he told her, allowing her to go first in to a large vestibule of the interior of the building.

A pretty woman broke out in a large smile, gliding over the floor with open arms. "Welcome to Wichita Falls," she told Charity. "I'm Lily." Instead of taking Charity's outstretched hand, Lily enfolded her in a sisterly embrace.

Charity seemed surprised at first then hugged her back. When Lily introduced Ben, her husband, he hugged her as well. It was interesting to watch her. They were the closest thing to family he had. This town, this life, he was building it together with all the people here. It made his past fade away as if he had never grown up an orphan.

Now she would become a part of this. At least he hoped she would. He had a feeling he had a fight on his hands. Charity Johnson was no pushover. She gave him a fire in his belly he wanted to claim as his own and he barely knew her for fifteen minutes.

He sucked in the sweet air the moment they left the hotel, letting it out in a long sigh.

Charity was beside him. "Want to back out?"

He leaned in, letting the warm air from his breath brush over her skin. "Not in a million years."

He grinned when he felt her shiver.

<> <>

This was not what she had planned on happening. Right before her, standing at the alter of this little church was the tall man she was about to marry. He was so horribly handsome it made her swoon. *Swoon!* The idea was utterly ridiculous and scandalous at the same time! When he lifted the hat from his head and faced her she got a better look at his face. A thin scar led a crooked pattern along his hairline, giving his already manly looks a dangerous appeal. Dark hair with hazel eyes that she had to look up to see stared back at her with amusement and seriousness at the same time. Was he as nervous as she? Charity had faced many men in her career without fear or trepidation. This man was a whole other story.

When he held out his hands she took them, imagining those strong hands and muscled arms around her. It was as if he could read her mind and by this simple action he was telling her everything would be okay. She blinked, looking at his chin instead of in his eyes else he would know what she was thinking. Was it wrong to have these kind of feelings for someone so suddenly. She knew the man for less than an hour!

Shuffling of feet stilled when Reverend Conners began to speak. His wife stood behind him, a small spray of flowers in her arms. The other witnesses, Lily and Ben Sloan, stood along side Ben's brother Dawson, who seemed jittery. Charity got the feeling he had other things to do besides stand over a marriage. She wished at times she wasn't so observant so she could pay attention to her wedding but curiosity always got the best of her.

The Reverend coughed. "Miss Johnson?"

She lifted her head to meet Daniel watching her. "I'm sorry, what did you say?"

The preacher's wife shifted behind him. Charity swore she heard a giggle but when she looked at the woman, her face was serious with eyes downcast. Although if she looked closely, the older woman's cheek kept twitching as if she were holding back a grin.

It put Charity at ease. Obviously, she wasn't the first bride to daydream in the middle of a ceremony.

Reverend Conner gave her the look. One that said to pay attention or the wedding was off. Even though he didn't say those words, she took the hint and lifted her shoulders.

"If you would please repeat after me, Miss Johnson, we can continue with this holy ceremony."

It was over before she could blink. When the preacher told Daniel he could kiss the bride, the man didn't hesitate but took a hold of her shoulders so quickly she was flung against his strong chest. She didn't have time to react when he dipped his head and kissed her like nobody's business. Claps began all around them. There was such a buzzing in her ears she didn't know where it was coming from. It was as if she were in a vortex of sounds that wouldn't end.

This was nonsense. He couldn't do this to her.

She pulled back and looked around, astounded. No one was paying attention to them but they were clapping and talking amongst themselves. So Charity did the only thing she could think of. She wrapped her arms around Daniel and laid a kiss on him to match the one she experienced a few seconds before.

It was powering to get such a response from him. He stilled at first, but when she deepened the kiss he placed his arms around her waist and bent her back. Her kiss backfired on her as he kissed her like he didn't care who watched.

Just as quickly he brought her upright, breaking the spell. The others laughed and clapped as the Reverend Conners shook hands with Daniel. He patted Charity on the shoulder but she didn't feel it one lick. The kiss had her in a state of mind as if she were walking on air.

Lily came up beside her and whispered. "Imagine what the rest of the night will be like if he's that frisky in public."

Charity's eyes widened. "I, oh!" She had to get it together. "It's not what you think," she whispered back, leaning closer so no one else would hear. "This is a business arrangement."

Lily laughed and gave Charity a hug. "Oh, darling, that's what everyone says at first. Then you get to kiss and make love and it all changes. I've loved Ben for years, told myself he was better off without me until one day I was enlightened to the truth."

Charity was intrigued. This could be another interesting story. "Oh? What is the truth?"

Lily smiled. "You will see, Mrs. Ashwood. Just wait and see."

A lady in a beautiful silk gown burst through the front door of the church. "Time's a wasting, the baby is on its way."

"Grace!" Dawson yelled out, turning in a frenzy and running from the building.

The others stood still for a moment before everyone began talking at once and tried to rush out the front door of the church. Daniel grabbed Charity's hand to pull her along. They let the door slam behind them as they followed the crowd to Dawson and Grace's house across the street. Everyone gathered in the front office where Dawson conducted business. He had a land office, along with his wife, who was obviously having a baby.

As the rest of the crowd paced, Charity felt the need to do something. She looked at Ruby, who took her hand, nodding as if she knew what Charity was thinking. They went through the back door, down a few steps and in through the kitchen of the attached house. The lady in the silk dress who burst into the church had an apron tied around her waist. She was standing in front of the fire, heating a pot of water. "You two came just in time. I need some help," she told them. "Grab those sheets and cut them in strips. Hurry."

Charity did as she was told, jumping right in and tearing the thin sheets, piling them on the table. Soon after, the older woman gathered them up to take them in to an adjoining room. When the screams began, she ran towards the door, wanting to help. The older woman came back out, holding up her hand to keep Charity out. "It is almost over, this is the worst part."

"Let me help. I learned a breathing technique that may help her." She didn't wait for an answer but opened the bedroom door to find two women in the room with Dawson's wife.

Sweat poured down Grace's face. She clenched her teeth so hard Charity swore she heard them chatter. She ran to the side of the bed and took the stranger's hand. Charity began to massage it, concentrating on getting the woman to focus. "Grace, listen to me," she told her, softly. The distressed woman looked over.

"Do I know you?"

"I'm afraid not. I'm a reporter, now married to Daniel Ashwood. But I did a story on this breathing method one time. It was amazing to see how it worked. Do exactly what I do, breath with me."

When Charity began to breath in and then as she let it out, used tiny puffs one after the other, Grace followed. At the peak of her contractions, she would look directly at Charity and get her breathing under control. When the midwife saw how it helped, she jumped in too, giving Charity a break. The other woman filled in when the midwife got tired. They worked as a team until the sounds of a tiny infant filled the air.

His cries rent the air so loud, it drew the attention of her husband who burst through the door unable to stay away a moment longer.

"Out you go, Mr. Sloan. It isn't proper to see her like this."

"I will not." Dawson leaned down and held his wife's cheeks in his hands. "I love you."

"Look what we have, a son."

Dawson's eyes widened when he heard it was a boy. Smiling, Charity tip-toed to the door, not wanting to disturb the life-changing scene in front of her.

Chapter 4

All eyes turned to Charity as she brushed her hands over her skirts when she entered the front office. Witnessing a baby in its infinite stage was breathtaking, short of a miracle. Someday she would put her thoughts on paper about this experience, even if it lasted but a few moments.

Daniel wrapped an arm around her waist. "You alright?" he asked, concern furrowing his brow.

She smiled up at him, glad for the strength of his arm to steady her. "I'm ready to go now." She was glad to have him by her side as they made their way through the crowded room. He seemed to take his job as her husband seriously. Even if it were a business arrangement.

The others begged her to spill the beans but Charity refused, telling everyone the family would be along shortly to announce the birth. She wasn't about to reveal anything, that was up to the parents.

Daniel didn't take his arm from her as they walked down the dusty road. Charity stumbled when she looked up to see the darkened sky. Tiny clusters of stars glistened above. They seemed so close, as if she could reach up and touch one. Her hand automatically went in the air and she giggled at herself for being so spontaneous. "The sky seems so much closer here than in Chicago."

Daniel grinned. "Trying to catch a shining star?"

"I suppose so. I have witnessed many things as a reporter in a big, bustling city but I was never a part of a tiny baby coming in to the world. I am amazed."

He stopped in the middle of the street. "Your eyes are glistening." Daniel stroked her smooth cheek with the back of his hand. "Your face, it shines with something tonight. It makes you look," he brought his mouth so close to her she leaned in to listen. "It makes you so vulnerable. I want to kiss you."

"Again?"

"If I may?"

She smiled then, her cheeks growing pinker. "You didn't ask in the church. You just took me, right there, with everyone's eyes on us as if no one in the room mattered."

"I'm sorry, you had me mesmerized. I am trying to be gentlemanly now."

"Maybe I don't want a gentleman." *Did she just admit that out loud?*

His brow shot up. Daniel made a sound low in his throat as he swooped down and crushed his mouth to hers. Her hands went around his neck.

"Not in the middle of the street, for cryin' out loud!"

Daniel reluctantly broke the kiss, but not before stirring a passion within her she had never in her life felt. "We were just married!"

"Don't matter. We's got to get a sheriff in this town, get rid of the riff-raff." The old man wore dirty pants, a raggedy vest over top a long sleeve shirt and a ragged hat. He shuffled down the street, a bottle in his hand, zig-zagging a bit before disappearing around the corner.

"Is he for real?" Charity asked, stepping away from Daniel to pull herself together. She kept forgetting their business arrangement. How impossible this was turning out to be! Perhaps she needed to remind him of their promise.

"That's Nate Jones, the official town drunk. Every night he staggers up the street with a bottle in his hand, hollering and yelling at anything that moves. I can see him from my desk through the big window in the newsroom. He never fails to pass by here."

Charity didn't realize they were so close to home. "We better get inside before someone else comes along."

Daniel helped her in, showing her the newsroom and his desk. He pushed aside some of the papers before offering her a seat.

"Thank-you, but I would like to turn in for the night. It's been a long day."

"Indeed." Daniel checked to make sure her trunks were upstairs, then led her up the steps to the second story apartment he told her was his quarters. She began to shiver half-way up the stairs.

"Dang-it, I forgot to close the window."

Charity looked around. It was a small apartment, the walls barren. A few pieces of furniture were haphazardly scattered around the room. A small table big enough for two was against the wall. She cocked her head to find a small flower in a single vase sitting in the middle of the table. The blood red rose was the most colorful thing in the place. It made her smile.

"You like my humble abode?"

Charity had to be honest. "It's in need of a woman's touch. Although the flower is a start."

He grinned. "Courtesy of a beautiful lady you will get to meet sometime. Mrs. Fisher takes care of her four grandchildren. She cleans to earn extra money. The flower was her doing. I'll still have her come each week, she needs the money."

Charity went to the cook stove sitting in the makeshift kitchen. The ashes were cold by now but there was a dish on the top, still warm to the touch. "Another of Mrs. Fisher's doings?"

"She had made dinner for us. Then the baby came, so we didn't get a chance to dine." He shrugged. "Are you hungry?"

"Starved."

"Yeah, me too."

"Let's eat." Charity took over, taking two plates from the shelf on the wall, setting them on the table. She found the silverware and placed them on a cloth napkin. Then before she had a chance to take the casserole dish from the stove top, Daniel reached out to help. His large hands picked up the dish and set it in the middle of the table.

"Thank you, sir."

"My pleasure. May I call you Charity?"

She set the cloth napkin over her lap. "I suppose so, but, only if I may call you Daniel."

"Of course. We're married, you know."

"Yes, a business arrangement. When do I start my job as your top reporter?" She grinned at the look of surprise on his face.

"Top reporter, eh? We'll see. Here, try some of Mrs. Fisher's casserole." He scooped a large spoon on to her plate and did the same for himself before lowering his head for a brief silent prayer. Charity dropped her chin as well.

When she looked up at him, Daniel was staring with those devilish hazel eyes. It took her back a moment and she swallowed. This had to stop. She was all business as she said sternly, "Daniel, you must stop giving me those looks."

"What looks?" he asked, his face so serious she wanted to reach across the table and touch his cheek.

"The one that tells me you want more than a business arrangement."

He sat back. "Things may be changing as we speak. I wasn't expecting you."

A shiver ran down her arms. She was having the same conclusion. Never in her life had she expected him to be so handsome, so forward and so, so, brutally honest with her. Most men she had met in the newspaper industry were out for one thing, themselves. She saw in the last few hours a man who cared about the town and the people who lived here. This was a whole new situation and she had to rethink everything now. "That works both ways, Daniel. I am pleasantly surprised myself." She had to be honest with him. "However, I am here to work."

"As I promised, you will be my partner in our business."

"Well, then, we must abide by our obligations. It's late. I would like to retire." She stood up quickly. His eyes were boring into her own.

"Perhaps you're right. This way." Daniel opened a small door to the bedroom where her trunks were lined up against the wall. He lit an oil lamp that sat on the table next to the large bed. By far it was the most plain and simple bedroom Charity ever witnessed. She would have to add a few touches here and there.

"I'll leave you now. Good night, Charity."

After removing her shoes and dress, Charity slipped a nightdress over her tired body. It felt so good to get out of her clothing and in something comfortable. Slipping under the covers, she leaning over and doused the oil lamp. Staring at the ceiling, sleep evaded her. Perhaps closing her eyes and counting sheep would do but every time she tried, all she saw were those hazel eyes burning into her own.

It was going to be a long, sleepless night.

<> <>

Daniel tossed and turned on the makeshift chair he used as a bed. He had waited until she turned out the lamp before he headed back downstairs to sit in his oversized office chair. As he watched the light dim from under the door of the bedroom, there was a bit of hope she would call for him.

She hadn't.

Charity was his wife in name only. She said that was what she wanted even if her words didn't correlate with her actions. A business relationship only. What had made him ask for something so stupid now that he realized she was the most gorgeous creature he had ever laid eyes on. In just a few hours he had decided she was honest and to the point, beautiful, and there was a desire to hold her in his arms and never let her go.

He stood up. This wouldn't do. How was he going to have a business only marriage to a beautiful woman who stopped the air from circulating when she was in the same room? Every single nerve ending would shatter if he had to spend too much time alone with her.

He needed a drink, even though he didn't drink. Daniel gazed out the large picture window to see the dim lights of the saloon still on. He checked his stop watch and realized it wasn't all that late after all. Closing the front door, he made his way to the saloon, needing to get out of there before he went stir crazy.

"What's your poison, newspaper man?"

Salem Nightingale polished a glass with a rag while he eyed Daniel. It wasn't too often he came in here but he knew Salem well. They had both been on the mercy train that night long ago. Salem didn't even know his real name. The two of them made it up on the long train ride west from signs that were pounded in to the ground on a long post. Kinda came close friends ever since, getting dropped off at Wichita Falls with two different families.

"Sasparilla."

The bar keep already had the glass ready for Daniel, knowing he wasn't a drinker. It wasn't that he didn't like the taste of liquor. Daniel was told his parents were both drunkards who left him on the porch of the old church long ago. It gave him a strong dislike of the stuff. But he liked to come here late at night when he couldn't sleep to talk to his friend.

Salem leaned his elbows on the wooden bar. "Got somethin' on yer mind, friend?"

"Seems so, Salem. Got married today."

"No kidding!" Daniel grunted when his friend looked around the saloon to see how many people were left this time of night. A half dozen men, along with one girl waiting tables were all that filled the room. "Next drink is on me," Salem shouted. "It's a celebration. The newspaper man, here, he done and got hitched!"

A hoop-hoop-hooray rent the air as Daniel laughed at the patrons making a ruckus. He took a long swig of his drink while the others worked their way up to the bar for their one free drink.

<> <>

Charity heard the soft sound of a door close. She threw the covers off and got to the window in time to see Daniel strolling down the street and disappear through the doors of the saloon. He seemed to be in a foul mood the way his shoulders were hunched down. Even so, he was a fine specimen to look at. Tall and handsome, why, any lady here in Wichita Falls would find him to their liking. Except she had to remind herself he was taken. Even if the marriage was a business arrangement, she wasn't about to share him with anyone. Why would a married man be out and about this time of night? Was there a story he was after? She wasn't about to let him get it all by himself. Not if she were to become the top female reporter in the territory. She'd have to be on her toes day and night apparently.

She found herself pushing the lid back to her trunk and digging through the container until she found her special disguise. As a reporter, she sometimes had to go undercover. Well, this was perhaps one time it paid off to purchase the things she did before packing her trunks.

The soft cotton material of the britches brushed against the skin on her legs. It was the first time she had to dress as a cowboy but in all fairness, Charity heard stories of how the west was wild and fearless and there was no way she could get around to the places she wanted to report on without hiding behind the pretence of being a man. The proprietor at the men's fine clothing store in Chicago told her that the britches, shirt and vest would help her fit in with everyone else. After donning the clothes, she grabbed a pair of gloves to hide her delicate hands and stuffed her long dark hair underneath a wide brimmed cowboy hat.

Charity worked her way downstairs, almost tumbling down the wooden steps several times. She wasn't used to wearing men's boots. They were bulky and with that spur on the heel made it hard to balance herself. She pushed the office door open and practised walking back and forth before leaving. At last realizing if she dipped her knees a bit, she could have better control of her walk. She had to look like a real cowboy.

Taking a deep breath, Charity made her way to the saloon. She bent down, picked up dirt from the street and began to rub it all over her face, trying to hide her womanly features. She brushed it over her gloves and pants, making it look as if she were a working cowboy.

The only thing she didn't have was a gun belt and pistol. Seemed like a bad idea anyway, since she didn't have a clue how to use a gun. With a giggle, she headed towards the saloon door. Charity wanted to experience the same things a man did. The fact Daniel was already there made her feel a lot braver than she was. The stories of the low-down dirty dealings in saloons made all the gossip trails even as far as Chicago.

Her boots hit the wooden porch. The soft strumming of a guitar seeped through the front door. Charity stood listening, her spur digging the soft wood and catching as she lifted her foot to take a step closer. A single thought occurred to her it may be a bad idea. Was she doing this as a reporter, to get the scoop on what it was like in a saloon? Or was she spying on her husband?

A little of both, she reasoned. He was her partner now, and yet she had absolutely no reason to doubt he was an upstanding citizen. He had proved himself earlier today at their wedding when they all ran to help while the baby was being born. It spoke volumes to his character.

Face the facts, Charity Johnson Ashwood. You are down-right curious what it's like in a saloon, a place where women are not welcomed. At least honorable women. Now, take yourself inside and be the brazen reporter you claim to be!

Those thoughts moved her through the door. The darkness of the room hit her square on and made her blink a few times until she could discern the figures inside. A few men played cards at a table in the rear. She looked to her left where a man sat by himself, his chin nodding towards his chest. A bottle teetered in his hand but each time she thought it would drop to the ground he jerked, lifted his chin and squinted.

Another man leaned against a far wall talking to the saloon girl. She had her hand on his chest making Charity unsure if she was pushing him away or holding on. A lone man sat on a stool strumming an old guitar. So far nothing major was taking place. This saloon was nothing like the stories she had read about. It was rather, demure, boring. She was here for the truth and took another step forward.

As she walked towards the bar she noticed a man leaning against it, his elbow on the top, his booted foot on the rail at the bottom. Charity eyed those familiar boots and worked her way up his tall body to stare at his back. It was Daniel, talking in quiet tones to a tall, muscular man leaning over behind the bar.

She steered away from Daniel, reminding herself to dip her knees a bit as she stopped further down, far enough away she wouldn't be recognized. She had kept the hat tilted low over her eyes in case anyone recognized her. Not that they would, she hadn't been in town more than a day at the most.

The bar-keep looked up. "What's yer poison?" he asked as if he said it a hundred times. Charity peeked out from under the brim of her hat as best she could. The tall man waited patiently, leaning with his elbow on the bar. She looked around. How was she supposed to know what to drink?

She tried to keep her voice low enough to sound like a man, yet it still back-fired, sounding more like a young boy who was going through the change. The high-pitched sound even caught the attention of the card players, who looked her way for a moment before their noses went back to the serious game at hand. "I'll have whatever he's drinking." She pointed to Daniel's glass.

"You sure about that?" He leaned closer to see under the brim of her hat. She tucked her chin against her chest even more.

"Yes, sir."

"Does your Pappa know you're out this time of night?" Salem asked.

Charity bit her lip so hard she winced. She wasn't fooling anyone but at least he didn't think she was a woman, but a young boy. "My Pa's dead." There, that should quiet his curiosity.

The bar-keep laughed in a low monotone. "What do you make of this one, newspaper man? Kid wants what your drinking."

Daniel slowly turned his head to stare at the cowboy. He didn't blink once or say anything for some time. Charity could feel those eyes on her, could imagine how he was looking at her outfit, sizing her up, staring at the cowboy boots on her feet. When he did look away, she released the air from her lungs. He didn't know.

She relaxed as he said, "By all means, give her what I'm drinking."

The bar-keep grinned and pushed a glass in front of her. Charity almost had the brim of the glass to her mouth when it occurred to her what he said.

She set down the glass. Turned her head to find Daniel staring with the biggest grin on his face. Anger reeled from under the brim of her cowboy hat all the way to the tips of her pointy boots. He knew! How was she supposed to investigate anything if she couldn't even fool a man who was practically a stranger? Her face fell as she turned away.

Had the newsmen in Chicago been right about her skills all along? Was she going after something so far out of her reach she was making a fool of herself?

Before she realized what happened, Daniel stood beside her, his boot on the rail below, a forearm on the bar. He fingered a coin, then she heard him say, "I'll bet your own by-line in the next paper you can't fool the men at the poker table."

Charity, shocked, didn't move a muscle. Was he going to give her a chance to prove she could get a story? It was a dream come true. Tilting her head slightly, she looked in his eyes to make sure he wasn't making fun, teasing her. "Anything I want to write about?"

He nodded once, his face serious.

"You're on," she told him, picking up the glass and downing it in one long gulp. Her eyes widened when she realized he was a fraud, too. A large grin covered her face. She shook her head before pushing away from the bar. "This won't take long."

An hour and a half later, Charity put a dainty glove-covered hand to her mouth to stifle a yawn. To everyone's amazement, she kept winning, one hand after another as if she were an expert. It wasn't really surprising to Charity, she had interviewed a man once who claimed to be a famous poker player. The report was never published but Charity learned a few card tricks which helped her with several winning hands tonight.

The others were disappointed the youngster was winning. All three of them kept pushing their luck, betting higher stakes than usual. "What did you say yer name was, boy?"

"Char, Ch, Charlie," she told them, yawning again. It had been a long night. Her lids were starting to droop at great intervals.

"Well, Charlie, don't be fallin' asleep. We plan to win some of our money back. I got me a fancy watch here I can put in the till if you all agree. Won it in Kansas City." After several murmurs from the others, he stared at the watch before relieving it from his wrist and set it in the pile.

Charity looked at Daniel, who was leaning on the bar, watching the game. Hadn't she proven herself yet? Not one of the men at the table thought she was anything more than a kid. That's what they'd say when she won a hand. *Look at that will ya, the snot-nosed kid won again.*

It was late, she wanted to go to bed. Then the thought occurred to her if she wanted to be a great reporter she would do whatever she had to for a story.

She forced herself to sit up straight. It only lasted so long though. After winning yet another hand, Charity's lids began to droop again. The voices at the table sounded so far away. Even the guitar music in the background petered out as she dozed off. It was getting too difficult to pay attention.

She swore she was flying through the air. When Charity opened her eyes everything was upside down. "Time to go, Charlie," he said. She found herself facing Daniels backside. Twisting her head, the men at the tables cried out.

"No way, man. We need the kid. Want to get my money back," the cowboy who lost his watch complained.

Daniel held her tight so she could take off her hat to gather up her money. She gathered it in her fists and placed her winnings in the hat. "You've just been fooled by a woman reporter, men. Here's the deal. I want to interview each one of you tomorrow at noon for a front page feature about cowboys and outlaws. If you show up on the porch of the newspaper, I'll give each one of you a fair share of your money back, including this watch."

"Interview? What for? Ain't nobody famous here."

"You will be," she told them, her head pounding from being held over his back like so. "Because tomorrow I'm beginning a four part series in the newspaper and you may just be the star."

"What! We already got fiction fodder. You sayin' we'll have more stories to read?"

"That's what I'm saying and you could be the star."

"Well, I'll be," one man cried out, excitement rippling through his drunken voice.

Daniel moved towards the door.

"Put me down!"

"Not yet," he told her.

"I'm wide awake now, Daniel, please."

"Jut a little longer, my sweet wife. I find I can't leave you on your feet for too long, otherwise you seem to find trouble all around."

She shook her head. "Oh, Daniel, I'm not trouble. Why not put me down and we can discuss this face to face. You can't possibly walk through town with me hanging over your shoulder like this!"

"I can and I plan to and then tuck you back in bed. This time I'm locking the door so you can't get out."

She laughed. His voice was not serious one bit. Daniel was fun to be with, that was for sure. When he realized she was dressed men's clothing at the bar, he had every right to get her out of the saloon and make her go home, being his wife and all. Yet, he made it a game, daring her to prove herself.

Was he interested in making her happy or trying to see how good of a reporter she could be?

This marriage was nothing like she expected. Even more so, when Daniel carried her all the way up the stairs and dumped her on the bed. He gave her a warm smile as he closed the bedroom door for the second time that night.

Chapter 5

Charity woke up with the sun shining through the window. It had to be late so she tore through her trunk to find a suitable dress to wear. She had four interviews today and needed to hurry. The clothes from the trunk were strewn over the bed but Charity ignored the mess as she made up her hair. It would wait. A bad trait of hers actually. Who had time to organize when there was a job to do?

The tiny bedroom she had shared with her room mate in Chicago was always a mess, mostly due to Charity. Every morning it had been the same. Waking up later than usual with clothes flying everywhere before running out the door, barely making it to work in time. She guessed that part of her life would never change.

Charity was surprised to find Daniel with his feet propped on the large work desk and his head tilted to one side, eyes closed. It stopped her in her tracks at his stoic appearance. He looked dead. She stared at his chest to see if it moved up and down. It was hard to see from across the room so she gently tip-toed to the edge of the desk, leaning in slowly so as not to startle him. She stared hard until she saw the steady movement before letting out the air in her own lungs she had suppressed.

A hand snaked out and pulled her on to his lap. Charity acted affronted at first, trying to pull away but soon gave up and began to giggle. She was learning never to take him for granted. Daniel was a constant surprise. "You haven't been to bed?"

"I haven't slept in that bed since I lived here," he admitted. "No time to sleep, I've got a paper to run."

She jumped from his lap, realizing she was feeling quite comfortable there. Taking a step back so he couldn't do that again, she told him, "I've been distracting you with this mail-order marriage. I'm ready to begin anew, let's get to work."

He showed her the press and the basics of the operation. Their heads low and serious, Charity realized the work here had to be tremendous for one person. To run the press and find things to report on was a lot of work. No wonder Daniel hadn't slept in his own bed ever.

She turned to him with a smile. "I'm here to help now, Daniel. Hopefully, you can relax a bit. I've got some great ideas I'd love to share with you."

"Hold on to those ideas."

Her face fell. Now he was going to tell her that her reporting didn't matter, she was a woman and there was no way he was going to let her have a by-line. Had it all been a lie? "You don't want to see my work?"

"You've got some interviews on the front porch."

She followed his line of vision to see all four of the men from the saloon making their way across the street towards the newspaper office. She hadn't expected all of them to appear. To be honest, she expected maybe one or two to show up.

But four! This was going to be a genuine interview and she was going to make it as professional as possible. Except her feet were frozen to the floor in shocked surprise.

"Go on," Daniel encouraged, as if he knew how nervous she was. He sat back down behind the desk, pushing his wire-framed glasses down his nose, acting as if he wasn't paying attention.

Charity was delighted. The man was giving her the space she needed and a chance to work while trying not to make her feel uncomfortable. He truly was different from the others in Chicago. She leaned across the edge of the desk and planted a kiss on his brow. "Thank you," she whispered.

She grabbed a high-back chair, placing it next to a lone stool. Hurrying back upstairs, Charity rummaged through her trunk to find a pencil and writing paper. She wanted to write down everything these men told her.

When she got to the bottom of the steps, Charity brushed her hand over a bunch of fly-a-way curls, patting them in place on her head.

She let the air fill her lungs, letting it out slowly. Swallowing and lifting her eyes to the top of the ceiling, she said a silent prayer to the man upstairs. *Let me conduct the best interviews of my life.*

For the next hour and forty-five minutes, Charity brought each man inside one by one, sitting them on the chair by the door and prodding them with questions. One of the men told her she was like a shotgun, loading and unloading in to him he couldn't answer fast enough.

Several grunts from Daniel when the cowboy complained had Charity sending daggers his way. Her stern look at his interruptions had him rolling his eyes and finally he got up and left the newsroom. Satisfied, Charity gave each man a share of their money back as promised. When the last man took a seat, she rubbed her eyes and took a quick look to see if Daniel made it back to his desk. The seat was empty.

Taking a deep breath, she stared at the man in front of her, sitting on the chair with his feet spread out. He wore a cowboy hat pushed back on his head. In polite society any gentleman would remove a hat before taking his seat. Not this fellow, there was something hard about him, as if there was a story brewing there. She stared at his hat and then looked in to his dark eyes. He seemed angry. With the right prodding, she may be able to get to the thick of things.

A lift of her brow while looking at his hat had the man making a funny noise. He reached up to remove it, apologizing in monotones, stuffing the hat between his thighs with a grin. "My apologies, ma'am. It's been awhile since I've been a gentleman. Usually out in the open, riding with men who don't make a matter if you remove your hat."

"Is that a fact, sir. Your name for my records, please?"

"It's Johnny. Johnny's all you need to know."

A skeptical brow was raised again. "Why is that?"

"What? Well, hell, girlie, I said I'd be interviewed for the notoriety but that don't mean you gotsta have my whole name."

She stared. This man had some deep secrets. Charity interviewed enough men in the small amount of time she was a reporter in Chicago and the tell-tale signs were written all over him. The way he fidgeted with his hat, a small trickle of sweat along his hairline. There was definitely something sinsiter or secretive going on.

She leaned forward. "How 'bout we call you Handsome Johnny, the mysterious outlaw from the Texas Plains?"

He lifted his head up, eyes widening. "Hm, well, I suppose so." A small blush reddened his cheeks at being called handsome. Charity bet no one ever called him anything nice before. He was far from handsome with rather large nostrils that made you look directly at it while speaking to him. She tried to avoid staring and kept her eye level to his. It didn't help that he kept lifting his chin in the air, forcing her to stare at two black holes with little tiny hairs sticking out. Charity bit back a grunt.

"Now, Handsome Johnny, let's get to the nitty gritty. Since we are writing true life stories with a flair for adventure, what details of your life can you tell me about? Have you ever done something you were sorry for? Where are you from?

She wrote as fast as the man could speak once he began to realize that she wanted sensational stories to put in the paper. He told her many things, his life running from the law, his work on a ranch right outside of Kansas city and his trek here to Wichita Falls.

"Is that it?"

"Well," he leaned closer, eyes darting back and forth even though no one else was in the newspaper room. "I rode with a gang of killers once."

The way he mentioned killers made her pause. The pencil stilled in her hand. "What kind of killers?"

He grinned, knowing he had her attention. The air was thick with anticipation.

Charity sucked in a deep breath. She was good at this, even better at getting confidential information than most reporters. "Is that all, killers? Like a gang, you mean?"

"A gang that's wanted around here, that's why I can't talk about it. If anyone finds out I rode with them, I'd be held for questioning, maybe even hanged. I left the night before the murders, before it happened. Wasn't gonna be part of that kind of killing. Left on good terms and was told I could ride with 'em anytime I wanted."

Charity stared at him. She picked up her pencil and shrugged. "No, that doesn't sound interesting at all. There are a dozen outlaw gangs from here to California. So many stories have been written about them I doubt we could use your story. That is, unless it was pertinent to this town."

Her voice held steady while her pulse throbbed against her skin. She had to have this story, instinct said it was bigger than anything she had ever written.

"Lady, I got news for you. I can give you the details of who started the fire down by the cabin along the creek here in Wichita Falls after they murdered two people. They've been searching for the outlaws for a long time."

Charity wasn't sure what he was talking about but it seemed important to the town. If he was telling the truth. "I'm thinkin' of catching up with them when they mosey on down here in a few days before heading to Mexico. There ain't much in this town I want anymore."

"So you are a true outlaw then?"

"Well, I guess you could say so," he bragged, his chest puffed out like a bull in a stall. "Except these boys, they are killers and I'm not. That's why I didn't follow when they were on their last spree. I stayed here and worked as a hired ranch hand. 'Cept I'm tired of working my fingers to the bone. Guess I'm more outlaw then I thought." He wrinkled his brows as if contemplating what he said, confused at his own words.

"Do you think I could get an interview with the leader of the gang?" She knew it was a longshot but had to ask.

Handsome Johnny slapped his thigh with the rim of his hat. "Oh, hell no, Zeek would, oh, I didnt' want to say his name. You don't go writing that down else I'll be dead meat, ya hear?"

His stare caused Charity to put her pencil down again. She didn't want to anger this man. He was going to get her an interview with a killer even if he wasn't aware yet. "I promise not to divulge any impertinent information."

"Make sure you don't, as a matter of fact, perhaps we should end this discussion. If I'm gonna go back to the gang, I sure as hang don't want you writing a story about us in the paper."

Charity stood when he did. "Look, Johnny. I can make you famous as a mysterious outlaw and no one knows your name or where you came from. I'll let you give me the details and I'll write the story."

He scratched his head. "Ain't that lyin?"

She almost smiled but didn't underestimate this man. He was valuable to her right now. As soon as she found out what gang he rode with, it could make her career. Especially if the gang was wanted across the territory.

"No, sir. Not lying. We're entertaining townsfolk. If I knew what gang you rode with, I could avoid mentioning them in the story." Charity tried to look confused.

It worked. He held up his hat, the brim covering his face even though no one stood ten feet from him. The other men interviewed were long gone. "That seems reasonable. Don't mention this name to anyone."

"Cross my heart." She made a production of crossing her chest with her hands, covering her mouth with her one hand pretending to cough. There was no way she would ruin things by letting him see her laugh.

"McKenzie."

In slow motion, she nodded. "Ok, but considering the circumstances, we should meet again until you meet up with this gang so I can get original material to use, even though we won't mention names."

He held out his hand. "Deal. See you tomorrow same time?"

Charity let out a big smile. "You bet, Johnny. I'll be right here on the front porch." She turned her head back and forth, pretending to be cautious. "We best not let my husband know we're in cohoots. He doesn't understand the type of story we are dealing with here. Let's meet at Jenna's at seven. I'll buy you a coffee for your time."

Charity shook her head smiling as the outlaw hurried across the street. When Daniel appeared from out of nowhere, she jumped and let out a gasp. "Oh, my! I thought you left, where did you come from?"

"I've been outside all along. You don't think I'd leave my wife in here alone with a man like that feller, do you?"

She smiled. Even though their whole marriage was a business arrangement, the beginnings of husbandly duty was starting to show. "That's sweet, Daniel. I doubt you needed to watch out for me." She gathered her notes together, placing them close to her bodice. "Do you have any idea of the seedy places I've been to in Chicago to get a story? Alone?" She didn't mention those stories were shot down by her rivals, never published.

He moved closer, his warm breath tantalizing her skin. "That ends now. You'll never have to worry about no protection. I take my job seriously, Charity." Her name coming off his lips made her pause. Did he know how he was affecting her senses?

"We're in this business arrangement," she said. Her voice was shaking.

"I know. Except I've been thinking perhaps we should take it a bit more seriously."

Charity stepped back, unable to think clearly with him so close. "I, uh, well, I think maybe we should get to know each other better."

He nodded. "You are right. That's why I made reservations for tonight."

"Reservations?" She wanted to find out who this McKenzie gang was and what happened here in town. Taking a look at back issues had been her agenda for the evening.

"At Jenna's Restaurant. Best place to eat in town."

"Probably the only place in town unless the hotel has an eatery?"

Daniel laughed. "Ben Sloan is a friend of mine. He owns the hotel. Hasn't put in a restaurant yet so Jenna's gets most of the business. I suppose when the town grows more, he'll put one in as well."

"That would be front page news then?" she asked, not knowing exactly what was in their paper. Perhaps it was time to do a bit of research. Then she could dig deeper for something on this gang.

"Everything is front page news," he laughed. "Perhaps after you've been here awhile, we can add another page to the paper."

"Thank you for the supper invitation, I'll go. Right now, I'd like to become familiar with the paper if you don't mind."

"By all means. I'll just run across to Jenna's and pick us up something light for lunch since neither one of us ate yet today."

Charity had forgotten about food. She never ate breakfast, although by noon her belly grumbled. Tons of coffee kept her going most of the day until she actually sat down to supper in the evening. In Chicago, she'd always stop at one of the little shops on her way to work or between assignments for a pastry to eat while working. It wasn't the healthiest way to live but such was the life of a reporter.

When Daniel returned, he spread out the bundle he carried in one hand on the top of the desk. Pushing away some papers, he opened the cloth to reveal a warm loaf of bread, along with two chunks of cheese. In the other hand, he carried a round tray with two cups of coffee.

The aroma of fresh coffee made Charity's belly growl. She giggled at the noise instead of pretending the sounds hadn't come from her.

"This will settle the stomach," Daniel said as he offered his seat to her.

"No, no. You sit. I'll bring a chair to the other side." She busied herself with the other chair while Daniel sat down. He cut a slice of warm bread for each of them. A small bowl covered by a cloth revealed butter that melted as soon as it met with the warm dough. He handed her several small slices of cheese as well.

"I'm afraid this is all Jenna had available. She closes from noon to three but when I explained we hadn't eaten all morning, she produced these goodies."

"Jenna sounds like a wonderful person."

"You'll meet her this evening at supper."

Charity glanced at a pile of old newspapers. "Do you mind if I go through some of these while we eat? I'd like to become familiar with the type of news we provide." Charity was used to doing several things at a time while she worked in Chicago.

"Help yourself. I have some advertisements to edit. Would you like cream in your coffee? I can run back as I forgot to get some."

"No, this is fine. Thank you, Daniel. This hits the spot." She gave him a genuine smile. Even though her heart was beginning to do some flip flops of its own in Daniel's presence, she had to keep her head on her shoulders. This was strickly business for now. If she didn't make a name for herself, the reporters in Chicago would be right. She would consider herself a failure.

Perhaps after she made it big then and only then would she consider a more serious relationship with Daniel.

The thought gave her more distress than she realized.

"Everything okay?" he asked, looking concerned. He stopped eating to watch her.

"I'm fine. Perhaps last night has worn me out." Although it was probably a silly thing to say. A reporter was always raring to be on the go, to get the news or story no matter how much sleep they had. She had to be careful what she said.

"We'll have no more of those late night shenanigans," he told her, a serious look on his face. "I don't want you hurt." His hand came out and covered hers. She held the cheese in her fingers, looking down at their hands.

It was nice to have someone looking out for her. A warmth rose inside of her that she had never felt in her life before. Was this love? Desire? Just as she pondered these run-a-way thoughts, Daniel plucked the piece of cheese from her fingers and put it in her mouth. Her eyes widened right before she bit down, causing her lips to touch the warm tips of his fingers.

He moved back, pulling his hand from her mouth. The eyes staring at her had a deep, wanton look. Even though Daniel didin't say a word, it was as if she knew exactly what he wanted.

This was not in the plans.

She brushed the back of a hand across her brow, pushing loose hair away from her forehead. Her nerves ran wild, causing deep shallow breathing to rise up. This had to stop, there was no way to be in the same room with Daniel and earn her way to the top if he caused her so much grief whenever he was in the room. "You have to stop doing those things to me," she whispered.

He didn't look up.

"Daniel."

He pushed back the chair. "I need some air. Carry on." That quickly he was out the door. She watched in confusion as he marched down the street in the direction of the hotel.

Oh, dear. Charity was in deep trouble. She began to flip through the newspapers trying to get her mind off of Daniel's gentle touch.

Impossible.

Then she kept telling herself she will never get to the top like this.

Maybe she should be a complete wife to him, let him finish whatever he seemed to start every time he was near.

Would it give her some type of relief so she could carry on her work?

She was indeed in big trouble.

Chapter 6

Daniel stomped through the hotel entrance like a man on a mission. Except there was no mission to accomplish. He had to get away from those deep sensual eyes that looked at him as if he were a man who could do no wrong.

"Well, what's gotten up your crawl this afternoon?" Ben asked, looking up from the boxes of books that were delivered a few minutes ago.

"Had to get away from the newsroom. A bit stuffy in there." His words were clipped. He didn't want to talk about Charity to anyone, except Ben's prying eyes said different.

"Could it be the bride has got you all full of angst this day?" Ben welcomed Daniel with a friendly nudge on his shoulder. He picked a book from the box and shoved it at Daniel. "If you came for a pity party, at least help." Two more books were thrown his way.

"What is it about women that makes a man want to stop dead in his tracks?" Daniel walked along side of Ben as they carried the books to the make-shift library.

"Lily makes me feel that way every single day. It's called love."

Daniel shrugged. "I doubt I love Charity. We haven't known each other long enough. She sure is spunky and makes me feel alive though, more so than I ever thought possible. You wouldn't believe, ah, never mind." He stopped talking the moment Lily came bursting in the room with another pile of books.

She stopped when she saw Ben wasn't alone. "Daniel, how are you? How is Charity getting along?"

"She is fine. Right now, she's finishing up some food and going through our old newspapers. Trying to familiarize herself with our town."

"Oh?" A troubled look came over Lily. She shuffled through the pile of books until she came across the one she wanted. Pulling it close, she nodded more to herself than anything. "The newspaper can't tell her anything that's imperative. I'll go on over there and I'm taking this Bret Harte book along. It's a view of the frontier by a San Francisco journalist. She'll need it to familiarize herself with the western world. I hear she's from Chicago."

Daniel grinned. Lily's tone made it sound as if Chicago was a foreign world somewhere across the continent. He watched as Ben took his wife's arm and pulled her close, giving her a quick kiss. "Enjoy yourself, my love."

She placed a hand on his cheek, kissing him back and smiling at him as if Daniel weren't there at all. Daniel had a deep desire for a relationship like that, he realized. One that made the world seem as if nothing was as important as the two of them. He ached for the kind of companionship they had, even if he tried to deny it over and over again.

"Bye for now, Daniel," Lily sang and waved before bustling through the door without a backward glance.

"Charity will be glad for the company."

She'll probably question Lily to no end. He knew there was something that was distracting her since she interviewed the last of her cowboys from the saloon earlier. He'd have to watch her closely. After all, she wanted to be the star reporter for his newspaper. That made people take chances that could be dangerous to themselves or others.

Daniel had a feeling Charity was about to become a handful.

"Why the long face, friend?"

"I'm not sure. Charity is up to something. She left Chicago, well, you read the letter. It was originally meant for you. Remember how you tried to make Lily jealous with a mail order bride?"

"Ah, that I did. Can't imagine where I'd be if I had actually gone through with the whole ordeal. I'd be one unhappy, miserable man." Ben grimaced.

"You are kidding, right? Lily would not tolerate another woman ten foot near you."

"Yeah, you are right there, old friend. Work calls for now but let's make it a point to get the women together more often. They could use some female companionship and I sure could use a card game."

Daniel recalled how the two of them, along with a few others in town would get together for a decent game of cards on a regular basis. They weren't drinking men, but it was a ways and means to unwind after a long day or week. Since Ben's brother Marshall had quit drinking, out of respect for him, the rest of the men didn't touch the stuff during their card games if Marshall was in attendance.

Since Lily and Ben got together and now had the hotel to renovate, the frequency of card games had diminished, almost non-existent. Plus, with Daniel the sole proprietor of the newspaper, he spent all of his waking hours catering to the whims and demands of advertisers and townsfolk.

Daniel ground his teeth. He wasn't complaining, he would never trade this life for anything. Images of his childhood were embedded in his brain. He'd never go back to living the lifestyle he came from. Hungry days, even hungrier nights. Starving himself in order to feed the younger children at the orphanage. It seemed like a hundred years ago and yet the events were embedded in his brain as if it had happened yesterday.

The positive thing was the couple who finished raising him when he got off the mercy train had been good to him even if they never gave him so much as a hug. What they did was to work him to the bone, the sole purpose of most pioneers that took in orphans. Yet, between the money he inherited and selling their house when they died, it was enough to buy the newspaper building. He was grateful for that at least. Unknowingly, his foster parents had made his long time dream of owning a newspaper come true.

The old man who owned the newspaper had hired Daniel twice a week to help with the newspaper business. His parents had obliged, letting him work there as long as it didn't affect his regular duties.

Daniel had followed instructions to a T, working hard and showing the old man he was listening even if long hours on the farm had him staying up twenty-four hours some days. It paid off in the end when the old man offered him the business first.

Daniel counted his blessings every day of his waking hours. Even if gut instinct told him trouble was brewing. He'd take that too before ever going back to the life of his empty and heartless youth.

"Help me get the rest of the books, Daniel, eh?" Ben slung an arm over his shoulder. They walked back in silence as he pondered what to do about Charity.

"I can't seem to keep my hands off of her."

Ben grinned. "That's a problem?" He shoved another box of books at Daniel.

"We have a business only relationship. She's told me several times and yet when we are together I get a feeling she wants more. I know I do."

"So, what's the problem?"

"I don't know. I think maybe we are wanting two different things. Charity's willing to be my wife in order to work as a reporter. In Chicago no one took her serious. It's her deepest desire right now, more important than anything else. She wants a career above being my wife. We knew and agreed on our terms from the beginning."

Ben looked confused. "Isn't that what you wanted? A partner to help you with the newspaper?"

"I guess I did. Except I didn't expect to get Charity."

"Sounds like you got more than you bargained for." Ben clapped him on the back.

"Yeah, I want to protect her, make her feel as if she's the most important woman in Wichita Falls."

"Yep, you got it bad."

"I won't smother her, it's not what she wants. Sake's alive, man. I am falling fast and hard here."

Ben roared. "Then go tell her."

Daniel shook his head. "It's too soon. Haven't known her that long. Maybe it's just a case of wanting to bed her. It's been a long time since I've been with a woman."

"Perhaps it's time you make her your wife in more than name only."

"I don't know. I best get back. Newspaper won't get finished on its own." Daniel left the hotel even worse off than when he got there. Confusion reared its ugly head as he contemplated what to do. Charity had his emotions in an uproar. On one hand she acted as if his touch was what she longed for and then she would gently remind him theirs was a business only arrangement.

Wouldn't do no good drowning himself in sorrow and worry. As he got closer, he saw Charity and Lily sitting at his desk, talking away like old friends. For some reason he didn't want to interrupt. Their heads were close together now reading something. He watched for another minute before turning away. From his standpoint, it looked as if Charity was digging up dirt on someone. She was doing more than familiarizing herself with the old papers. That much he knew from years of people watching as a reporter.

Suspicion grew inside his gut. What was she looking for? Ever since the interviews earlier he could tell she had her mind on something. It was a reporters anxiety. He knew. Daniel had been in those shoes many times. He turned towards the saloon. If the last man she interviewed was anywhere this time of day, it was in the saloon. Time for a Sasparilla.

Daniel pushed open the doors to the saloon. He blinked harshly so his eyes could adjust to the darkness of the room. Several men were already there, drowning themselves in drink. He spotted one of the men who had been interviewed by Charity leaning against the bar, his back to the door. Daniel moved closer, nodding his head to Salem for a drink. He stayed far enough away so as not to get in the man's space after realizing it was the last man Charity had interviewed.

"Here's your poison," Salem mumbled. Daniel picked up the mug, leaning his booted foot on the rail below as he took a deep slug.

No one but Daniel and Salem knew he didn't imbibe alcohol. Salem knew Daniel's history, how his parent's abandoned him on the church steps, loving their drinking more than him. It messed him up for years, made him an angry child. He swore he'd never become like his natural parents. So far he had kept his promise.

Now, along comes Charity and messes up his mind more. Maybe a real drink would help. He almost told Salem to pour him a shot of real whiskey until the man next to him poked him in the ribs.

"You that newspaperman?"

Daniel nodded. "Yep." He set his glass down, glancing over.

The scruffy man smirked. "Well, guess I'ma gonna be in your paper. That wife of yours is gonna write a tale about Handsome Johnny. Yeah, that's me, it'd be good for you all to remember."

"Handsome Johnny, eh?"

"That's right. Can't say no more. My lips are sealed."

Daniel looked at Salem, who was looking from one to the other. His brow went in the air as if in question.

"Is that a fact?" Daniel told the man. "Can't say what your story is gonna be about?"

The man shook his head back and forth so vehemently he almost knocked his drink from the bar. He stopped it from toppling with his hand. "Nope. Promised not to tell, or to die-vulge where we'll be meeting to finish up the story so don't ask."

Daniel rubbed his chin. What was she up to? "You talking about meeting in an undisclosed location?"

" Dis-what? Nope, meeting at Jen-ah, nope, can't tell ya! Now don't go asking no more." He deliberately turned his back to Daniel.

Salem grinned. "Looks like you got some reporting to do. On your wife."

"Seems so," Daniel agreed. "I think I'll keep what I know to myself, see how this pans out."

Daniel knew she was aching to get a good story. All he could do at this point was to sit back and see what she was up to. One of the men, probably the one in the saloon here, told her something. He had a bad feeling in the pit of his gut. He regretted allowing her to interview the men at the poker table. They were mostly men with lower standards. There was no way he was about to let her out of his line of vision now.

By allowing her to come in to her own, he may well be putting her in danger.

Daniel didn't plan to stop her from meeting up with Johnny but he wouldn't be far behind. He, too, knew how to disguise himself.

<> <>

"It's nice to get out for supper. Thank you, Daniel."

Daniel smiled. "Your welcome. Right this way," he told her, opening the door of Jenna's Restaurant. A young woman in a black gown clapped and welcomed them.

"Jenna, this is my wife, Charity Johnson Ashwood."

The dark-haired young woman's brow rose. "Oh? How lovely. Welcome to Wichita Falls, Mrs. Ashwood."

"Please, call me Charity." She held out her hand so the other woman had no choice but to take a hold of her own. Charity wanted to make it clear to everyone she met that she was an independent woman no matter that she was married to the newspaperman. In her observing of the opposite sex, Charity always found the wife stood behind the husband as if she were of no importance.

Not Charity. She stood beside Daniel, her head held proud and her eyes directly on the person she spoke to. She would never be a little scared mouse. It wasn't in her nature no matter what polite society dictated.

"So pleased to meet you, Charity." The genuine smile reached Jenna's eyes. She placed a menu on the table. "Will you have the house wine?"

Both Daniel and Charity nodded. "I'll make an exception for tonight," he told Jenna but his eyes were on Charity. It made her nervous.

"I'm sorry, you don't drink wine?" It was the two of them at the round table, set back in a romantic corner of the room. A single candle flickered from the middle of the table.

"No. Tonight I make an exception." He shifted his chair closer.

"We can drink something else," she offered. "I don't drink wine often."

"I don't drink it at all. However, I think it's time we celebrate our union."

Charity wasn't sure what he meant by those words. The heat coming from his side of the table was about to make her sizzle. She picked up the menu to take a look. Daniel leaned in.

The way her stomach was churning tonight she doubted she could eat a bite of food. This man had her in a tizzy. She sat back and sighed. "Daniel, you are doing it again."

It didn't stop him, made him get closer to her. Next thing she knew his warm breath was closing in, she felt it on her cheek. "I'm mad about you."

What could she say to that? She had to stop this now. "Daniel, I, uh, I came here to Wichita Falls to work. You're making things difficult for me to concentrate."

Her eyelids fluttered as she looked at her hands, clutched so tight together on the round table in front of her. He laid a hand over top, his gentle, warm hand causing her to take shallow breaths. Where was the air when she needed some?

"I'm sorry. You are right." He moved back, pushing his chair further away. "I get carried away when you are near me. You do look so lovely tonight, I'm afraid I lost my mind for a moment."

She smiled. "You sure know how to charm a lady, sir."

He grinned before releasing a long sigh. "At any rate, you are right. I'm sorry to put you on the spot, Charity. Let's have a nice, relaxing dinner."

After that, they ordered their meal. While waiting, Daniel filled their glasses with wine. As she sipped, Charity watched Daniel. He wrapped his fingers around the wine glass, tilting the liquid for a few moments before raising the glass. It was like watching him in slow motion. For some reason, Charity thought he was fighting some inner battle that kept him from taking the first sip. She looked down at her own glass, half empty. If she kept drinking like this she'd be drunk as a skunk before their dinner came. A giggle erupted.

Daniel set down the glass. Charity noted he never took a sip. "What's so funny?"

"I'm not even sure why I laughed." Her fingers went to cover her mouth. A tiny hiccup emerged and she giggled again.

"You getting drunk on a half glass of wine?" he asked, amusement ripping through his tone.

"I suppose I am. I hope they hurry with our meal."

"It won't be long. Eating something solid will help some, I'm sure."

"Oh, Daniel, you are so sweet to me. Thank you for this nice dinner." She went to pick up her glass when his own hand stopped her. She stared at the stark contrast. His was so much larger and darker than her own pale skin.

"Stop that," Daniel told her, his voice low.

"What am I doing?" she whispered. The feel of his hand on hers made her breathless.

"Your tongue. Keep it in your mouth. I won't be able to stop from kissing you if you don't stop licking your lips."

Charity pulled her hand away, embarrassed. "I am so sorry." She grabbed the napkin and dabbed her mouth where she realized the moment he touched her hand she had been licking her lips in an unladylike fashion.

Jenna returned with their plates of food. "Here you go." Placing them on the table, she asked if they would like more wine.

"I'll have a Sasparilla instead."

Jenna didn't say anything, perhaps she already knew about Daniel's aversion to alcohol. "Would you like another glass then, Charity."

She looked at Daniel. For some reason he was staring down the bottle of wine. "No, please take the bottle from our table. Perhaps one of your other patrons would like to have it instead. I'll take a Sasparilla, too."

Daniel's head jerked up. His dark eyes stared in to hers. When she saw the look on his face it occurred to her that his soul was tortured. She hadn't been able to put her finger on it before, but now seeing it so clearly made her want to touch his face, to reach out and tell him that everything was okay.

Charity was never one to keep silent. "What happened, Daniel? Why don't you drink alcohol?"

Jenna dropped off two glasses of Sasparilla. Charity took a sip the same time Daniel did and they smiled at each other. He set his down.

"My parents, whoever they are, left me on the front porch of an orphanage in New York City when I was two. When I turned six my mother came back for me. She was always drinking, leaving me home alone. My dad was so drunk he couldn't even talk, only hit me when I tried to talk to him. I wanted to go back to the orphanage. At least I didn't have to be alone."

Charity knew not to interrupt or else she would lose him. Her silence prompted him to go on.

"I ran away several times, wound up at the orphanage but as long as my parents were able to take care of me, I had to go back to them. We lived in a tiny apartment, it was so crowded I had to sleep on a blanket in the corner. My parents wouldn't stop drinking not even after he lost his job at the boat docks. That was the beginning of the end. They got kicked out and had no place to go. We slept under bridges and in places I can't tell you for some time until one night my mom and dad never came back for me. I found my way to the orphanage alone. Six weeks later I found out they were killed trying to steal food."

"I'm so sorry," she whispered.

"They chose to drink over me."

She didn't have any words to say. He was right. "Let's eat before our food gets cold."

They ate in silence. Charity knew Daniel was living his childhood over again. If she could take away his pain, she would. Did that mean she was falling in love with him? What did it mean? She didn't want to have these type of feelings for this man. All she had wanted was to do a job, become a star reporter and live her life without any issues.

Here she was, sitting across a table from a man who was starting to peck away at her heartstrings.

She was in deep trouble.

Chapter 7

Charity was back at Jenna's to meet with Handsome Johnny. She wore a plain calico patterned gown today with a large broad-rimmed hat to hide her face. No sense letting everyone know she was consorting with an almost outlaw in bright daylight. Looking around, she noted most of the others were eating a hardy breakfast but she sipped on a cup of coffee.

Johnny hadn't shown yet. Was he going to show up? She drummed her fingers on the table in anticipation. Charity needed him to be here. Without his directions, she'd never find the outlaws. She had her suspicions on what murder he was talking about but she needed to hear it from him. As a reporter, she wasn't about to accuse anyone of anything unless she had proof of the matter.

The sound of talking and laughter filled the air. Almost full, Jenna's was the place where everyone went for breakfast. Her expert eye followed four men sitting at a round table, gobbling down food so fast it made her head spin. No sooner had the last one set down his fork, chairs squealed as they got up and threw money in the center of the table before exiting.

Charity watched a loner at a corner table, his cowboy boots the only thing she could make out. A newspaper covered his upper half. She grinned. Come Monday, she was sure there would be a much bigger story than what was keeping him so occupied.

She knew exactly when Handsome Johnny made his way to her table. Sitting down, he ordered a cup of coffee and breakfast. She watched in silence as he gobbled down the food as if he hadn't eaten all day. After a few minutes, his head came up. "You payin' for this, right?"

Charity raised a brow. "I suppose I am." She hadn't planned on more than a coffe but if doing got the information needed then she would.

"I figured so. Now, let me see what kind of story I can tell you today. Oh, hey, how about the time I almost got myself kilt on -"

"I would much rather hear about the McKenzie Gang."

"Sh, don't talk so loud," he muttered. His eyes moved around the eatery, searching for, what? Charity almost burst out laughing, she doubted any gang member was sitting in this restaurant.

"Spill your guts, Handsome Johnny, I don't have time to dally. The paper has to be printed and out by Monday. That leaves four days to write up this story and get it to the press. I need your cooperation."

"Four days you say. Welp, gonna meet up with my pals on the morrow. Dang it, I didn't want to say that too loud." He leaned his upper half over the table between them, his crusty breath making her almost gag. She took the napkin from her lap and dabbed it over her mouth to keep from breathing in his stale breath.

"Your meeting the *gang* tomorrow? Let me come with you, do an interview." Charity's heart rate went up. This would be her ticket to notoriety.

"No dice, girly! There's no way they'd take to a woman reporter."

"What if I find a man to do the interview? Would you reconsider?" He squirmed in his seat a bit.

She noticed and took advantage that he was uncomfortable. "That is, if you actually know this so called gang. For all I know you could be making this up, after all, I am a stranger to this area."

She watched him inhale through his nostrils and those beady eyes open wide. "What's that you say? You don't know squat! Why, I do too know the McKenzie gang," he said, his voice carrying through the eatery. "Dang it!" Johnny scraped his chair back and stood. "Now look what you've done, made me say their name out loud for all the world to hear. The deals off!"

"Wait! We never had a deal. Unless, you want to prove to me you do know them? Imagine your name, Handsome Johnny written in bold letters on the front page. I can make sure a man is there to interview in the morning. Where shall we meet?"

Johnny chewed on his bottom lip. Charity knew he wanted the interview, wanted the fame of knowing an outlaw gang even if he was trying to hide the fact. He twirled his hat in his hands while contemplating her offer.

He took a step back then leaned close to her ear. "Sunlight, down by the river where the old cabin stood. The place where the murders happened."

Charity stiffened. "Murders?" She knew which murders he was talking about.

"That's right, the murders. Make sure you are there by sunrise and there's a man reporter. Pretty sure if anyone see's you, I'm afraid you'll never make it out alive."

She tried not to show any fear. Little did he know Charity planned to be the one to interview the gang. She hadn't brought cowboy costumes for nothing.

After Johnny left, Charity paid the bill and got up to go. The place was pretty empty by then, the only other customer the man behind the newspaper. She walked by him, her sharp eye noticing he hadn't taken his eye off the newspaper. "If you like reading our newspaper, wait until you see Monday's paper. You may want to make sure you get an early copy."

When the man didn't react except for a grunt, she moved along, out the door and back to the newsroom. She had a lot of preparation to do for the meeting in the morning. Excitement ran through her. She wanted to skip across the street but didn't dare. No one could know she was about to meet the outlaws who murdered the wife and child of one of their townsfolk. If she were able to find out where they were heading, the possibility of killing two birds with one stone would raise her to the top of her profession.

<> <>

The newspaper dropped to the table. Daniel stared at the back of Charity's simple calico dress. The wide-brimmed hat was low on her head, as if she were trying not to be noticed. He grunted. How could anyone not notice her fine attributes to that plain looking garment. It didn't look so plain the way she wore it, the curves of her body shaping it nicely. He had to get his head on straight no matter how fine she looked.

Unable to hear their whole conversation, Daniel did hear the McKenzie gang mentioned. Handsome Johnny's horrified look made him grin. Charity was good at getting information from others, that much he could tell. Whatever the man had told her, she was on a mission to get a headlining story.

Standing up, he ran his finger along the handlebar moustache he wore in case she happened to get a closer look at him. He hadn't wanted her to know he had been here when the place opened, waiting patiently for the two of them to arrive. After reading between the lines while talking to Johnny in the saloon, he knew it had to be Jenna's place they were going to meet at. He ripped the thing from his face and handed the cowboy hat to the kid clearing the tables. "Here ya go, son. One cowboy hat for letting me in first thing."

"Thanks, Mr. Ashwood. Have yourself a fine day."

"Indeed, same to you."

Daniel was expecting Thomas, his new apprentice to stop by later in the day. The first job he'd give him would be to keep an eye on Charity while he followed Johnny to see if he could figure out what the outlaw was up to. He made his way back to the newsroom to find Charity pacing back and forth.

"Good morning, Charity. What has you so excited this morning?"

She stopped pacing. Twisted her fingers. The nervousness oozed from her. "I, uh, nothing."

Daniel took his seat behind his desk. He tried to ignore her pacing but soon put the pencil down to stare once again. "Charity!"

Again, her pacing stopped. She looked back at Daniel surprised he was even in the room. Her mind was severely distracted, that much he was sure of.

He opened a top drawer in his desk and took out some coins. Before she could start pacing again, Daniel moved quickly in front of her. She stepped back as if surprised he could move so fast. "Here," he told her, placing the coins in her open palm.

"What's the money for?" Her brow creased, confusion rippled across her face.

"A shower."

"What?" She sniffed the air.

He laughed. "It's not what you think. Go to the Hotel. Today is Tuesday."

"Which means what?"

"Ben put in showers at the hotel. Every Tuesday the townsfolk can get a shower."

"I've never had a shower before. I've heard of them, you know, living in the big city and all."

"I would like you to report on them for next weeks newspaper release."

She looked incredulous. "You want me to report on a shower? You're kidding me, right?"

"Now, look. I know you are wanting to do a great story but everyone has to start somewhere. We have to do the regular stories as well as the headliners."

Her eyes were on him, suspicion shooting from those beautiful blues. "Why don't you do it?"

"Because I've already had a shower. I want it from a woman's point of view."

Exasperated, Charity spit out under her breath, "This is not what I signed up for."

"If it makes you feel better, I'm going over to Weaver's Mill, going to report on the smell that is permeating from an area in the back near the outhouse. Would you care to switch with me?"

Charity grinned. "I'm sorry. You are right, we have to report on all the news, even if it is downright silly. Thanks for reminding me."

Daniel went to take a step towards her before realizing it wouldn't help to get himself too close. "Go on, now. There will be plenty of time to get the big stories."

She scurried upstairs for a change of clothes. As she was leaving, Charity turned to him. "I am going to enjoy this, even if it is a strange story to write about."

Daniel looked up as if he weren't interested in what she was doing. "Don't forget to ask for the lavender soap."

Charity smiled wide. "Thank you, Daniel. That's kind of you to take my needs into consideration." She closed the door quietly.

Daniel sat back in his chair, staring out the window as she made her way towards the hotel.

<> <>

Charity was glad now that Daniel gave her the assignment of the hotel's shower even if it distracted her from the investigation in to the McKenzie Gang. At first she thought he was trying to keep her distracted, knowing she was up to something. It didn't help he was so smart. The man had a way of searching your soul and knowing exactly what was inside.

Her new friend Lily told her to meet her in the library after her experience in the shower. Charity took one last look around, embedding the experience in her mind before finding her way to the hotel's new library.

"Lily."

The dark haired lady looked up and smiled. Charity liked her from the moment she met her the first day she got here. It was nice to have someone who was as determined as her to get through a man's world.

She had a hunch Lily had led a hard, tough life before finding solace in the arms of her husband.

"How was your shower?"

"Refreshing to say the least. I love the smell of this flowery soap."

"Ah, yes, the lavender. It is quite fancy and so strong. Your husband will be able to smell you coming a mile away."

Her words stopped Charity in her tracks. It was no accident Daniel wanted her to experience the lavender soap. He knew she was investigating something, but wasn't sure what. The man was smart. Too smart. She tapped her finger over the side of her cheek, contemplating how to get rid of the smell so he couldn't follow her. He may be smart but she wasn't going to let anything get in her way of interviewing this outlaw gang. "Maybe it's too strong. How in the world do I get rid of this strong smell?"

"Why, Charity. You want to encourage him, don't you?"

"Not at all. We have a business arrangement. I don't want his paws all over me, it's awful. I can barely stand to have him touch me like he tries to."

Her words weren't true. She had a hard time lying about his touch but was desperate now to get rid of the fragrant smell of lavender that would lead him right to her. When Charity looked at Lily's face she knew someone was behind her. She was afraid to turn her head because the eyes of her friend told her everything.

Gathering courage she swung around. Daniel's angry, hurt eyes were on her. Scenes of his childhood, how his parents threw him away, preferring alcohol over a child flashed through her mind. Now she was doing the same. Choosing to get a famous outlaw gang's story over his feelings. It was cruel and yet their arrangement was business. Strictly business. Agreed upon in two mail-order letters from the beginning of this arrangement.

Daniel turned and walked out the door. He hadn't said a word. From behind her, Lily sighed. "Now you did it, Charity. I've never seen Daniel so angry before."

She closed her eyes. "I've hurt him. I didn't mean those things I said. It was, oh, he tricked me."

Lily came up behind her and draped an arm across her shoulder. "We better have a glass of wine. I'm afraid you are going to need it to get through this one."

The two had a glass of wine in the library as Charity admitted her true feelings for Daniel. "The honest truth is I walk in to a room and he makes me feel as if I am the only person in the world for him. I get all goose-bumpy and my heart beats from my chest so fast I can't breathe. Can I have another glass?"

Lily poured them each another one. Charity drank half of it in one gulp. Her lips were loosening up. She should be out there, researching the McKenzie gang, not holed up in the hotel talking about how Daniel excites her.

Lily giggled. "I think we're getting tipsy. My husband will have my hide," she told Charity. Yet there was a devilment in her eyes as if she had every intention of looking forward to her husband's wrath.

Charity wished she had a relationship like that with Daniel. Except theirs was strictly business. She shook her head, trying hard to remember. Her head began to thump at the memory of how he looked, the anger and hurt at her words making her feel like a real heel. "I have to apologize."

Lily nodded. "Go on then, go find Daniel. I'll hold down the fort here." She giggled again, going off in search of her husband. As Charity made her way to the front of the hotel, she heard the two laughing. In the foyer, a smiling Ben had Lily in his arms, carrying her up the flight of stairs. She doubted they even saw her as she walked by.

Outside, she brought her hand up to cover her eyes from the warm sun beating down. Charity had left her wide-brimmed hat back in the library and wasn't about to go get the overbearing thing. It was a beautiful day out. She lifted her face to the sky and laughed out loud. Most women wore a hat to keep from getting too much sun. Today would be different. She had two glasses of wine and was feeling mighty fine. Silly even.

Stumbling down the street, she wasn't ready to go home. Perhaps a walk would do her good. She shouldn't have drank two glasses but she did.

Charity wasn't too drunk to notice a young man following her out the corner of her eye. When he got a bit too close, she stopped and turned, putting a look of horror on his face. "Why are you following me?" she asked, closing in on the boy.

He backed up. "I, uh, I work for Mr. Ashwood."

She raised a brow. "Is that so? Pray tell, what kind of job does he have you doing?"

The boy shuffled his feet. He was maybe fifteen at the most. "I, uh, I am his apprentice. I can't tell you my assignment."

Since the boy was taller than her, Charity lifted her chin in the air. "Young man, does that assignment have anything to do with following me?"

Her words were getting a little slurred. She regretted drinking. It wasn't like her to do so but Daniel had her mind too worked up lately. It was his fault, she tried to tell herself.

"Uh, I can't tell you, ma'am. I'm sorry." The boy stood his ground. He would make a good reporter someday.

"What's your name, son?"

"Thomas."

"Well, Thomas. Here's a new assignment. You go back to Mr. Ashwood and tell him that I'm on to him." She crossed her arms over her stomach. "If he continues to harass me in the streets, I'll file a lawsuit against him."

Thomas looked at her, his face incredulous. "You can't file a lawsuit against your own husband. It's against the law."

"It is?"

"It most certainly is. I'm afraid you would be a laughing stock of the town."

She swayed back and forth, reaching out for the rail along the side of the street where travelers tied their horses. She felt a bit steadier hanging on to the wood. It would have to do until she sobered up enough to walk back to the newsroom. "Well, you go on now and tell him my exact words. I'll be home soon, you tell him that, too."

When the boy didn't nudge, she lifted her arm and waved it around. "Go on now, hurry. He should know I know about this assignment."

"I was told to stay with you, ma'am. If I leave you, I would fail at my job."

"Hm, you have a point." She put her finger against her mouth. "Here's the thing, Thomas. You got caught. I'm sure you were supposed to keep an eye on me without me noticing, correct?" At his guilty nod, she smiled. "The fact is if you don't go tell your boss what happened it may be worse for you. I like you, Thomas. I want you to continue to work for my husband's business. But, frankly, I caught you so you best go on back and report it to your boss. I'll wait right here until you do."

Thomas nodded. "I didn't think of it like that. Okay, ma'am, promise to wait right here?"

The moment she nodded, Thomas took off down the street like a pack of wild horses were after him. Charity lifted her skirts and crossed the street, a little wobbly. Miss Addie looked up from where she was bent over on her porch, clipping the stems from a few roses she picked. "Mrs. Ashwood, is that you?"

"Yes, hello, Miss Addie. May I ask a favor please? Do you mind if I go inside to sit a spell? I promise not to bother you while you are doing your task. I need to, um, prove a point to someone."

"Why, of course. Are you well?" Miss Addie took Charity's arm to help her up the two steps to her house.

"I was visiting Lily."

She didn't need to finish her sentence when Miss Addie quipped, "She got out her bottle of wine, no?"

"She did. I'm afraid I had one too many. This is not how I behave at all."

Miss Addie helped her inside the parlor, settling her on the settee. "Lily bought two cases of wine from a peddler that claimed it was from the vineyards of Italy. Turns out after some investigation from Ben's part, there is no such vineyard in Europe. A local man from Dallas was trying to sell it as a world renowned wine. Needless to say, Ben refused to sell it in his hotel so Lily is handing out glasses to anyone who enters her library."

Charity laughed. "It is certainly working, even if the wine isn't world renowned. It's very tasty."

"It must be for you to imbibe so freely."

"I'm sorry, Miss Addie, I didn't meant to intrude. If I may rest for awhile, I'll be out of your hair soon."

"Am I to understand you would rather not let your husband see you intoxicated?"

"No. I am hiding from him because he thinks I'm up to something."

A confused look came over Miss Addie. "I don't believe I understand."

"He has hired an apprentice."

"Yes, young Thomas. I was speaking to him on his way to the job. That doesn't explain why you are hiding out."

Charity sat back in the cushions. Miss Addie's couch was so cozy. "I was the job. He was hired to follow me."

Miss Addie raised a brow. "Oh? Is there a reason you should not be trusted, Mrs. Ashwood?"

She giggled. "Yes. Most certainly. I'm a reporter. I plan on becoming the best woman reporter in the west." Her eyelids were getting heavy. A nice rest would be wonderful, she thought, but, Miss Addie kept talking so much.

"I think I'm seeing the whole picture now. Mr. Ashwood is worried you may get yourself in to some trouble now."

"Kind of already have." Charity yawned.

"Are you hiding from Mr. Ashwood?"

"I most certainly am."

Chapter 8

Daniel hurried down the street, his body alert, eyes on everything that moved. She was not leaning up against the wooden post across the street from Miss Addie's boarding house as Thomas mentioned. The kid had a lot of learning to do. Charity coerced the young man to believe what she wanted him too. Had to admit, she was clever.

Even so, he wasn't about to let her go off and interview the McKenzie Gang on her own. Not as long as he had any breath in his body. For that matter, this incredulous idea of hers may well get her killed.

If he hadn't cornered Handsome Johnny and made him spill his guts, she would be going off in the early hours of the morning to the creek, the same place two resident's of Wichita Falls got murdered a few years back.

Daniel would make sure she got her story but she would learn one thing, it took more than one person some times to get the leading story of a lifetime. He wasn't about to let her go it alone. No way. That's why he told Johnny the deal was off unless he came along. Johnny had no choice but to agree after realizing there would be no front news article unless Daniel approved.

The only way Daniel would approve was if Charity was in a safe and uncompromising position. It was why he was about to change the whole interview process. She was going to fight him on this, he knew. Even if his touch made her cringe.

He'd bet she made that part up too, even if he heard her with his own ears. She had been planning this assignment all along. It was what she wanted. She'd get what she wanted. He'd give her the glory and then he'd see if she still couldn't stand his touch.

Somehow he doubted his touch made her cringe.

Because she melted in his arms whenever they were in the same room together.

They were meant to be together. It was inevitable. Their lives were about to change. She was going to get it all, a leading story and a husband who wanted her deep down from the bottom of his core.

He stomped across the street, stopping in front of Miss Addie's bed and breakfast. "She here?"

Miss Addie didn't look up from her task. "Yes, Mr. Ashwood, she certainly is."

"Are you going to stop me from taking her home?"

"Certainly not. She is however, resting for a spell. May I call on you to come back in a few hours?"

"That would depend on the fact she doesn't try to leave here. I'll sit for a spell if you don't mind."

Miss Addie shook her head. "I'm afraid you may be sitting for quite some time. She had two glasses of Lily's wine."

"Two!"

"I'm afraid so."

"That explains a lot."

"She'll be fine here. Come back in two hours."

Daniel agreed. Turning on his heels he headed back towards the newsroom. First, he needed to stop and notify a few others about tomorrow morning's activities.

<> <>

Charity woke up in a strange parlor, forgetting for a moment she had gone to Miss Addie's for a spell. Leaning forward on the settee, she peeked through the sheer curtains to find Miss Addie and Daniel on the porch, conversing. Her head didn't hurt as bad as she thought it would after two glasses of Lily's wine, which surprised her. Getting up though was a lot harder than not. She teetered back and forth until she found her footing. Smoothing her skirts, she tip-toed closer to the front door, standing there for a moment before opening. The two talked too quiet for her to hear what they said.

"Come on out, Charity."

She stepped on to the wooden porch, hanging on to the porch rail. Daniel instantly stood, taking long steps to reach her, putting an arm around her waist. He didn't say a word about the harsh words he overheard her say at the hotel. All he seemed to care about was her state of mind.

"Now don't worry none, Charity. We'll stop by Jenna's for something to eat, it will make you feel a whole lot better."

"I'm not sure I can eat."

Miss Addie smiled. "I've had an interesting afternoon. Now if you don't mind, I'd like to retire to my house guests." Addie had a working bed and breakfast. She took her work seriously to make sure all guests were comfortable and entertained well. Some days she would play the piano for their enjoyment, other times have a social where she invited members of the town to join in.

Charity turned to Miss Addie. "Thank you so much for your hospitality. I'm not sure how I would've gotten through the afternoon without your help."

"No worries, Mrs. Ashwood. Good evening."

The walk through town to Jenna's Restaurant was quiet. Charity didn't want to talk. She liked that Daniel kept his arm around her waist, guiding her down the street, avoiding pits in the road and steering her away from places she didn't dare step. She felt safe. Safe in his arms.

She shouldn't feel that way, after all, they were business partners. Even though he wanted more. Charity should apologize for what she said earlier. "I didn't mean those harsh words, Daniel. I truly didn't mean to say those things."

He didn't reply, instead, guided her towards the front door of the restaurant. A crowd gathered outside, waiting to be called in. "It looks packed tonight. Do you mind waiting?"

"Not at all. My stomach is beginning to grumble a bit. I guess I'm hungrier than what I thought."

"Wait here. I'll go let Jenna know we want a table." He disappeared inside the building while she waited in line. He didn't say anything when she apologized. Did it mean he was going to forgive her? The fact is he made her feel more alive than she ever had felt in her entire life. Her whole world came alive at his mere touch.

It had been a long day. She wanted to eat and go to bed so she could rest up for t he big day tomorrow. Getting the story of a lifetime was the reason she was here, in the west, in Wichita Falls.

When the door opened and Daniel walked towards her, she realized how lucky she was. This man was her husband, a gentle, kind and loving man who had given her an opportunity to better herself. He was nothing like those reporters in Chicago. He never once degraded her or made her feel as if she weren't good enough for the job. Charity realized she was falling hard. Fast. There was no stopping her intense feelings for this man.

"Ben and Lily have a table. We can join them and won't have to wait in line." He held out his arm to her, grinning. "After you."

She followed him to their table, where he held a chair for her. Guilt reddened her cheeks when she said hello to Lily. Daniel was being so nice to her and she had told Lily she couldn't stand to have him touch her. She had to clear the air. She coughed, gaining everyone's attention. "I'm going to come right out and apologize."

"Whatever for?" Lily said sweetly.

Charity looked at Daniel when she spoke. "For speaking ill of my husband to you, Lily. It simply isn't true."

Lily coughed. Charity swore she heard a light giggle. "It's quite alright, Charity. We had a bit too much to drink, didn't we? I should apologize for pouring you a second glass but I just love the wine and to share it with others. Perhaps I should give it all away right now since it seems to cause me trouble."

Ben shook his head. "No. I like when you drink the wine."

Lily's smile was so wide it made Charity laugh as she watched the two exchange a look. She took her eyes from the couple to watch Daniel. He had been gazing at her while she watched the two. Now he stared outright, grinning. "I'm not sure I like my wife drinking the wine."

Charity smiled back. "I am sorry about what I said, truly. Please, forgive me." She placed a hand over his, wanting him to believe her. She may want to be the best reporter in the west but her feelings for the man in front of her were coming in at a close second. In a way, the idea of being the frontrunner of the newspaper was taking a close second to him.

Was she in love?

Impossible!

Charity realized she couldn't wait to be alone with Daniel. As their dinner came to an end, the two couples hugged and went their own ways. Charity had been waiting to announce to Daniel her plans. She tightened her hand on his arm, which slowed him down for a moment.

"Everything okay?" he asked.

"Fine, Daniel."

"You certain? You seem occupied about something."

The only thing she was occupied with was the fact she had made a major decision while at dinner. "Yes, I believe you are right. It has everything to do with you. Us."

He stopped walking and turned to her. "What is it?"

"I want to be your wife." There. She said the words he wanted to hear.

Daniel looked dazed. Confused. His mind seemed occupied as well tonight. Perhaps it was bad timing. Except Charity wasn't one to pussyfoot around. When a decision was made, her idea was to jump in full force and get through things.

Daniel's reaction was startling. She tried to back away from him but his hand reached out. "Do you mean those words?"

"I, yes. I do." Her voice wavered. This was a big rule change. "I want to show you I don't mind your touch."

Daniel tilted his head. "Charity," he said, his voice low, strained. "You don't have to prove anything to me. I know you weren't serious. As a matter of fact, I'm inclined to believe you were saying those words to convince yourself more than anyone. Am I right?"

She nodded. "Can we go inside?"

People were walking by them as they stood face to face along the side of the street. The sky was beginning to darken as the sun rode low on the horizon. Charity wanted this. She wanted to be loved by Daniel. Tonight.

In the morning, she wasn't sure what the outlaws would do. The uneasiness in the pit of her stomach when she thought about them was real. What if she didn't make it back? Was she chancing fate by going out on a limb, hiding in disguise to get a story? At least she had tonight. Charity wanted to know what it was like to be in his arms.

His hands cupped her cheeks, pulling her to him while his mouth covered hers in a gentle, tender kiss. Her pulse thickened. Charity's knees began to buckle. It happened every single time he touched her.

The walk to the newspaper seemed to take forever. Daniel would stop, turn and kiss her so tenderly it made her shudder inside. Then he would pull her along, holding her up while they took another ten steps until he turned one final time and crushed his lips against hers. She pulled away. "We better go inside. I see the drunk coming our way."

They laughed and ran towards the door, sliding inside right as the old town drunk came around the corner. Luckily, he never noticed the two. Daniel gazed in to her eyes. "Are you sure, Charity?"

She smiled. Nodded her head, taking a long, deep breath. Then she took him by the hand, kissing his lips softly before going up the stairs. "I've never been more sure of anything in my life."

Daniel followed, mesmerized, closing the door firmly behind him.

<> <>

A rooster crowed somewhere outside. Charity snuggled against the warmth of his body, smiling when she realized it was Daniel's strong arm around her. She shook herself awake, not wanting to get out of bed but aware that in just a few hours, her whole world could simply change. For worse or better.

She was in dire need of a new plan. Charity had let her heart lead her last night, even though she was so happy right now. But it was time to meet Handsome Johnny. She wanted the story, didn't she?

Sliding in slow motion from under the sheets, Charity was careful not to wake Daniel. She gazed back to find his eyes closed, a steady movement as his chest rose while he slept. Tip-toeing across the room, she opened her trunk to find the cowboy outfit at the top. She was glad she wouldn't have to dig through the piles of clothing, making more noise than necessary. .

Hopefully, she'd be back before he woke up. The shades of early morning sky wreaked havoc across the sky. In a while it would be daylight, so she had to keep moving. Charity hadn't expected for Daniel to be in her bed so she went down to the newsroom to dress. After securing her hat and the dark gloves to hide her feminine fingers, she closed the front door to the newspaper and fled towards the saloon where Handsome Johnny promised to meet her.

When she got there, he was standing outside, smoking a stale cigar. The smoke billowed around his face, causing him to gag and cough. She got a whiff of the tepid smoke and choked back a dainty sneeze. Charity took the bandana from around her neck and placed it over her lower face to cover her nose and mouth. It made it easier to stand being in such close proximity to the outlaw. As they worked their way across town, she followed him while he guided his horse. All of a sudden he stopped. "Now listen, missy. I have to go in first so you gonna have to hide behind one of the trees I tell ya to so I can talk to the McKenzie's before I go taking you in there. They'll shoot first and ask questions later if I go in with someone they don't know."

She nodded. The closer they were getting to the river, the more her stomach began to quench. It felt as if a fist were squeezing her from the inside out. Was she crazy to do this? The path he led her down was winding its way further from town towards the river. She took a chance to look back. The town seemed forlorn, too quiet this time of the morning.

Charity was unsure now. She wanted to be brave but was this the way to go about getting a story? Did she want to be number one so bad she'd risk her life like this? Before it didn't matter, she had such a driving force to prove herself. But that was when she was alone in the world. Now she loved someone. Someone who was a part of her. She was a wife. Charity wanted to be a mother someday, didn't she? It seemed that her whole life of wanting to be a top reporter to prove the men in Chicago wrong didn't matter as much now. What if she didn't make it out of here alive?

When someone rode up behind them the hairs on her neck stood up. She jumped, slamming her hand across her mouth so as not to cry out. Her first instinct was to run. Instead, she whipped herself around to face whoever was coming up behind them to find Daniel there. "What in the world are you doing here?" she questioned sternly while at the same time a wave of relief broke through her. Her nerves were shattered with every step she took closer to the water and the sharp voices heard in the distance.

The river was just over a small ridge. She turned to Daniel. "How did you know we were here?"

When she saw the guilty look on Handsome Johnny's face, she stopped walking.

"Now, Charity, don't go getting upset. I forced Johnny to spill the beans." He slid off his horse. "It's out of our hands." He kissed her cheek, working his way to the opposite side of her face where Johnny couldn't see what he was saying to her. "Things are going to get downright ugly in about thirty seconds. When you hear the first shout, I want you to get behind that tree."

She stiffened. "I'm not going to get my story, am I?"

"Not right now, Charity. I promise you'll get it before the day is over. Please." His warm breath made her lean in to him even if they were about to be immersed in the center of a dangerous situation.

The long, drawn out shout came, drawing attention from the outlaws on the other side of the ridge. Charity turned to run, knowing she had to follow instructions this time. "It's okay," she shouted to Daniel. "Be safe. I don't care about the story. I need you to be safe."

He galloped after Handsome Johnny, who realized he'd been duped when he saw a large body of riders charging towards the river. It looked as if half the townsfolk were heading there. Shots were fired while Charity hid behind a thick oak tree, her back against the hard bark, both hands over her ears. With her heart thumping against her chest, she squeezed both eyes closed, praying to God Daniel wouldn't be hit. After a few minutes, she slid to the ground, careful not to move where anyone could see her silhouette. Shaking, she twisted to the right, afraid to move but wanting to know if Daniel was alive.

To her relief she saw him on the horse, a rifle slung over his shoulder. Funny that she hadn't noticed the shotgun when he rode up to her earlier. All she had noticed then was his masculine frame and how his warm breath had made her heart race. The shooting had stopped. Looking around, Charity could see two of the outlaws lying on the ground, their bodies riddled with bullet holes. She ran out from behind the tree towards Daniel. He turned and saw her, sliding from his horse and taking long strides to reach her. His arms wrapped around her, holding her close.

"I'm so glad you are safe." Pressing in to him, Charity knew this was where she wanted to be. Yes, she wanted to cover the biggest story ever but without Daniel, nothing would matter much.

"Thank you for listening and staying behind the tree." He leaned down and covered her mouth in another one of his tender kisses.

When Daniel let her go, she took her hand and placed it on his cheek. "Thank you, Daniel. I'm so lucky to have you."

He grinned. "You still want a story?"

"I sure do."

"Follow me. I think there's someone you want to talk to."

Charity ran to keep up with Daniel as he led her to the two outlaws who were on their knees on the ground by the river. Both their hands were tied behind their backs while blood seeped from one of the men's forehead. Daniel pointed. "That's Zach McKenzie. I promised you a front page by-line. Go get your story, Mrs. Ashwood, the most famous woman reporter on the Texas Prairie."

Charity dug deep in her pocket for her paper and pencil. She would write the best front page story ever.

Chapter 9

The Town of Wichita Falls Captures Infamous McKenzie Gang! by Charity Ashwood. A single tear slipped down Charity's face. This was the one thing she longed for, a by-line on the front page of a newspaper.

Strong arms came around her from behind. "Congratulations, Mrs. Ashwood. You did it." He nuzzled her neck, dropping small kisses against her tender skin. She leaned into him.

"We did it, Daniel. You. Me. The town." She turned in his arms, wrapping her own hands around his neck and securing a long, drawn out kiss. As she looked up, his hazel eyes stared out the big picture window. He smiled.

"I think we have an audience."

She turned. There was a crowd across the street, waving and clapping, some throwing a fist in the air. They all had just received their copy of the weekly news. The townsfolk were ecstatic the outlaws were brought to justice.

"Your name is becoming famous around these parts," Daniel told her, his gentle hands massaging her tired shoulders. She had spent the last few days and nights working on the article. Newspapers all over the territory picked up the story, bragging about one of their own, a brave and daring newswoman who infiltrated an outlaw gang for a story.

"I'm hoping this news reaches as far as Chicago," Daniel told her. "Serves them right to hear they lost the best reporter they had."

She shrugged. "Their loss, Daniel. Let's go join the others."

Hand in hand they walked across the street to the joyful cries of the townsfolk. After securing the outlaws on a stagecoach with armed guards, they were taken to Dallas, where the two would be held in the county jail until their trial. Since Wichita Falls had no jail or sheriff, justice had to be served somewhere else.They were lucky the town of Wichita Falls didn't serve out their own justice.

"Perhaps it's time we build a jail house," someone mentioned.

Ben nodded. "I'll foot the bill. Wife's an accountant, you know. She's got some extra money tucked away we'll never use."

"Guess we should hire us a sheriff, too."

Charity chimed in. "I think perhaps we should form a committee to vote and make some changes in our town, what do you think?"

Daniel agreed. "I'll keep everyone informed of the process by a weekly column."

Murmurs, head nodding and outright hollering came from the crowd. Daniel and Charity gazed lovingly at each other. She wanted him all to herself. "It's been a long day, husband. I'm going to retire."

"Not without me," he told her, gathering her in his arms as they walked back to their newspaper.

Changes were coming. But first, they were going to love each other until the morning light.

<u>2 months later</u>

"Charity! I've got a letter for you." Thomas came bustling in the newspaper filled with excitement. He'd proven to be such an asset to the newspaper by helping with everything. He wasn't afraid to get his hands dirty. The young man learned quickly and was heading for a great career in journalism.

Charity reached for the letter, her brows coming together when she saw the return signature. Chicago Tribune stood out on the envelope like a dirty mud puddle in the middle of the road. Fear and trepidation made her react as if the letter was a snake ready to strike. She set it on the desk, staring hard.

"Well, aren't ya going to open it up?"

"Oh, Thomas. I'm not sure I should."

"Go on. At least see what it says."

The idea of an apology from Barry or Jimmy burned in her soul but if she opened it up she would know for sure. She paced back and forth across the room, unsure. Did she want to open this back up? After the outlaws were captured, Charity realized she didn't want the life of a notorious newswoman in a bustling city. She was loved in this small town, with a husband who adored her more than life itself. As she did him. The people were kind, hard-working and made her feel as if she were a part of something. She hadn't felt that way in Chicago.

In Chicago, she was another journalist, trying to find a place in a man's world.

She stood in front of the letter. After ten minutes of staring at the envelope, she picked it up and stared some more. Her curiosity got the best of her. Thomas began to talk to someone but she wasn't paying attention. Charity felt the air as the front door opened but still she continued to stare at the envelope.

When she picked it up, she turned it over, biting her bottom lip. In a way she wasn't surprised if it was an offer to come back to the Tribune. After all, she held her ground, proved herself as a reporter. The thought of those two men apologizing was a great feeling. The thought of a job offer was horrifying.

She'd be a fool to turn down a notorious newspaper like the Chicago Tribune. It would sky-rocket her career to a level like no other.

A rough voice whispered in her ear. "You won't know unless you open it, darling."

"I am afraid. It's scary."

"I'm here with you." His gentle touch against the small of her back gave her the courage to slide the letter opener and rip the top off. Unfolding the letter, she read silently to herself.

She began to cry. Tears slid down her face, unashamed. She began to choke on her sobs. She let the letter fall and held her hands over her face.

Her husband stiffened.

He seemed so angry without saying a word.

She turned to face him but he walked away, out the door, slamming the door hard.

"Wait!"

He didn't turn around. Walked down the street straight into the saloon.

Daniel thought she was crying for all the wrong reasons.

She secured the cowboy hat and heavy boots before looking out the door. The townsfolk were in their homes for the night. It was late and Daniel hadn't left the saloon since he walked away in a huff earlier. If he had waited she would have explained her outrageous behavior.

Now she was about to put all of this to rest once and for all. When he found out the real news he would be so ashamed. Surprised.

With a smile on her face, she practically danced down the street. The old town drunk came around the corner just as she was about to step on the boarded walk. He stopped dead in his tracks and stared hard. "You a lass?"

She grinned.

"Well, I'll be darned. Strangest thing I've ever seen." He shook his head back and forth as if he were dreaming. Looking down at the bottle in his hand, he mumbled to himself that maybe he'd been drinking way too long.

Charity laughed and walked inside. The dark interior made her blink several times. She lowered the cowboy hat even more, working her way to the bar. It was a bit more crowded in here tonight but she was determined to get Daniel's attention one way or another.

She spotted him at his regular place at the bar, his booted foot propped on the lower bar. With an elbow leaning on the top of the bar, he twirled his glass of Sasparilla in his hand, staring at the bottles lined up on the shelves.

He never noticed when she sidled up alongside of him. Salem came over to her, recognition on his face. "What's yer poison?"

She grinned. "I'll have what he's having?"

"You sure about that?" Salem muttered, a jovial smile penetrating from his tall frame.

"Sure am."

Daniel slowly turned his head. When their eyes locked, the torture on his face made her cry out. She realized right then he had been scared she would leave him. She saw the pain in his eyes that led to his soul, the part where he had been abandoned as a young child. How could she have forgotten what he had gone through before? She needed to reassure him.

Charity picked up the Sasparilla and took a sip. "I'm not going anywhere."

She heard his sharp intake. "I'm stuck with you, then?"

She laughed out loud, the feminine sound turning heads close by. "You sure are, Mr. Ashwood. For life."

"Yeah?"

"Yes. The letter was an affirmation, Daniel. An apology and a request to work with them. An offer to fire Jimmy if I came back."

"How can you pass this up?" He put the glass to his lips and took a long draw. Charity noticed how he clenched the glass with an iron fist.

"I've gotten a better offer."

He turned to her. "What? Where?" Anger began to seep into his voice.

She flung her head back and laughed, almost knocking the cowboy hat from her head. "Mr. Ashwood, I got the best offer of all. Motherhood."

Daniel stilled. "No kidding?"

She waited. Knew it was coming. Then it happened. A wild, crazy sound erupted from deep in Daniel's chest. He picked her up in the air and held her close, her legs dangling. Small kisses covered her face and neck. "I love you, Charity."

She gathered his face in her hands. "I love you, Daniel."

Their kiss deepened and some serious heckling began. "What's he doing kissin' a young boy?" someone hollered.

"Disgusting!"

"Why, that's unheard of in these parts!"

Charity and Daniel laughed. He pulled her hat off and threw it in the air. Her silky hair fell from atop her head, falling in long streams down her back.

"That ain't no boy, it's a daggone woman!"

"A woman!"

"Holy mackerel!"

"Let's get out of here," Daniel told her, picking her up and carrying her out of the saloon. "It's time we have a proper honeymoon."

"You're not going to carry me all the way back to the newsroom, are you?"

He kissed her again. "I sure am."

Townsfolk were still out in the early evening hours. They stopped to stare at the two carrying on in the middle of the street. "People are seriously watching us," Charity told him, while dropping small kisses across his face.

"We're having a baby!" he shouted. "A baby! Did you all hear!"

When they got back to the newspaper, a fancy buggy waited out front. Daniel held on to Charity, who insisted on being put down. "Not on your life, darling."

She hung on to his neck while he spoke to the stranger.

The gentleman stood with his hat in his hands. "You Daniel Ashwood, newspaper man?"

"That's right. I'm kinda busy at the moment."

"I'm wanting to put an advertisement in the paper."

"It'll have to wait until morning. Shops closed." Charity noticed the man was well dressed. His buggy was fancy, nothing like it in the area.

"Okay. I'll be back first thing in the morning, then."

Daniel stared after the man as he crawled up in his buggy, taking the reins in his left hand.

"Where you from, stranger?"

"Wont' be a stranger for long. Name's Max Ward. I'm here to settle Byron Ward's matters."

Daniel held his breath. He nodded to the man. "Come by any time after daylight. Goodnight."

"Who is he? I heard your long sigh when he said his name."

Daniel smiled. "Nothing gets by you, does it, newspaper woman? Forget about Ward. Let's go inside. I want to show you something."

"What do you want to show me?" she asked, her eyes dancing.

"How much I love and adore you, Mrs. Ashwood. You've changed my life."

She pulled him down for a long kiss. "You changed mine, Mr. Ashwood. Forever."

*****

Thank you for reading Daniel and Charity's story. Don't leave yet, there's so much more! Meet the next bride, Hannah.....

Do you remember Lily and Ben's story and the run in they had with Byron Ward in book 3? If not, there was a mean, nasty rich rancher who almost had Ben killed and bullied Lily. Well, did you know Byron Ward had a son?
Can the sins of the father be redeemed? Or, will the whole town of Wichita Falls shun them?
Find out in the next book!

Hannah is Now Available on Amazon![1]

(https://www.amazon.com/Hannah-Order-Brides-Wichita-Falls-

---

1. https://www.amazon.com/Hannah-Order-Brides-Wichita-

Falls-ebook/dp/B01H0PPAXE/ref=sr_1_1?s=digital-

ebook/dp/B01H0PPAXE/ref=sr_1_1?s=digital-

text&ie=UTF8&qid=1487865589&sr=1-

1&keywords=hannah+mail+order+brides+of+wichita+falls)

Or, if you'd like to read the whole Volume 1 in one shot, get a boxed set Available now!

Mail Order Brides of Wichita Falls Box Set Volume 1[2] (https://www.amazon.com/gp/product/ B076YXYBN8)

---

2. https://www.amazon.com/gp/product/B076FYXYBN8

Cyndi Raye Reading Book Order

Books by Cyndi Raye
    Mail Order Brides of Wichita Falls Series
    Ruby
    Grace
    Lily
    Charity
    Hannah
    Rebecca
    Sophie
    Ellie
    Jenna
    Leila
    Boxed Set Vol 1-8
    Christmas in Wichita Falls Holiday Book
    Brides of Mill Ridge Series
    An Outlaws Honor
    A Reverend's Rose
    The Ranger's Redemption
    A Doctor's Devotion
    A Teacher's Treasure
    A Sister's Sanctuary
    Sons of Nora White Series
    A Bride for Luke
    A Bride for Adam
    A Bride for Samuel
    A Groom for Nora
    A Bride for Russell
    A Bride for Wesley
    A Groom for Widow Young
    Multi-Author Series Contributions

A Bride for Abel - The Proxy Brides Book #4
A Tin Star for Christmas - The Belles of Wyoming
Candy Cane Christmas - Ornamental Matchmaker Book #10

All these books and more can be found by visiting
https://www.amazon.com/Cyndi-Raye/e/B00ENA1WEG

Don't miss out!

Visit the website below and you can sign up to receive emails whenever Cyndi Raye publishes a new book. There's no charge and no obligation.

https://books2read.com/r/B-A-PXQ-OFMFC

BOOKS 2 READ

Connecting independent readers to independent writers.